In My Eternity

In My
Eternity

Ujjawal Pahwa

PARTRIDGE

To order additional copies of this book, contact
Partridge India
000 800 10062 62
orders.india@partridgepublishing.com

www.partridgepublishing.com/india

Contents

Author's Note... ix
Acknowledgement.. xi
Preface xiii

Chapter 1   Dramatic Arrival... 1
Chapter 2   Stepping Stone... 6
Chapter 3   An Inquisitive Teen.....................................14
Chapter 4   Magic!...18
Chapter 5   Debacles.. 28
Chapter 6   The Void.. 39
Chapter 7   Last Days of Summer................................. 47
Chapter 8   The Twists and Turns of Life..................... 56
Chapter 9   Teenybopper... 69
Chapter 10   She or 12ᵗʰ Boards?!...................................81
Chapter 11   Moments under the Sun 88
Chapter 12   Trauma... 94
Chapter 13   The God's Call...107
Chapter 14   The Warmth 113
Chapter 15   Kiarra 119
Chapter 16   Chaos!..132
Chapter 17   Are you happy? 147
Chapter 18   18!..160
Chapter 19   Eternities 170

About the Author..183

In the memory of my cousin brother.

I Miss You and I Love You.

Author's Note

So before you read some of my fascinating instances let me take a point of my life for you and thank you for choosing this pile of pages, I am sure you will be able to relate yourself with the characters while reading this novel. I came in contact with my life when I failed to get admission in St. Xavier's College. It is where I grabbed the opportunity to share my story. Why? The answer is just simple, I too had one. We all have a past, no matter how did it go. Just go back and see how it was and trace it out of your heart; link your past with today. Join me as I walk through the pages of this novel.

With Love

Preface

That day I bid farewell to one of my classmates at the airport. I saw the plane fly over my head and I said him good bye. I could have been a part of the journey too, but perhaps God had some different plans for me.

I sat alone on the lake throwing pebbles until the sun vanished. I found my position trouncing as the sun set under the horizon. On the way back home I stopped at her place.

"Ma'am what should I do, English has ruined it all." I handed her my result. "An aggregate of 95 in all and 84 in English" My dream of getting into DU was shattered.

"Tell me one thing, why did you left Christ?" I was fed up to answer this question. It was thrown at my face from every corner in those days.

"I wanted to move to Mumbai. I didn't like Bangalore; food and all."

"And you have nothing now? What plans next?"

"Indore!" I sighed, never wanting to use that word. I was just hoping for some miracle to happen. Every time I talked about my college with anyone, I cursed myself for leaving Christ University on the first place and not preparing for entrance tests of the other colleges.

She went inside the Kitchen to fetch some snacks for me. We sat and talked. "I have tried everywhere."

"Don't worry you can again try in the next year. Till then build yourself."

"Build myself?" She nodded.

"I didn't get you." I gave a despaired look at her.

"A diamond cuts a diamond, remember that." She convoluted the whole thing for me. I sat silently, face palming.

"If English has ruined it, let English decide things."

"Ma'am please!" I still didn't have the faintest idea of what she was talking about.

"You will have to improve your English. The best way to do is to"

"Join English Classes?" I intervened. She gave me a small pat on the head.

"First of all, Read! Pick up anything and Read, In spite of interest. Just read and find meanings of the words and phrases you don't understand. Strengthen your vocabulary." She said.

"Secondly, write about yourself. It's the only thing you have your best command over and that is indeed the thing you can do impeccably."

"What would I write?"

She gave herself a food of thought and continued. "Scrutinize your life. Know from where it all began and where it has come to. Go back to your childhood. Know what Ujjawal was back then and who he is today."

I hummed, biting the cookie.

In My Eternity

"I'll help you out, just give it a start. Go home, grab a pen and notebook, and begin from today itself."

"Okay I'll give it a try."

From that night, I sat down to write my diary. Oblivious to what the pages would hold months later, I just began to pen down all what I knew about my life.

3 Months Later

She opened the door. I surprised her by handing her my diary with pages filled up to more than half of it. She read my diary the same day and messaged me in the middle of the night "Do you want to be a writer?"

Her benevolence found my lost spark. This was what I needed. Exactly this! Somebody who would not find faults in the blunders I did earlier, somebody who would tell me that flaws are incomplete voids that can be filled in with optimism and good things. And all good things take time. To find the lost hope in the eternity of my life, I am writing this pile of pages. I hope you find yours.

Chapter 1

Dramatic Arrival

Aah! She screamed. "I can't bear this pain anymore lets go to the Doctor." At midnight he hurried to take an auto rickshaw. It was not an ordinary kind of pain but a pain rather more sweet all Women bear it in their life time. She was pregnant.

There were heavy rains outside and the water had completely covered the road, chilly winds had already lowered the temperature.

Indore hadn't experienced rains in mid Jan in the last couple of decades but today was something unlike.

He came back wet coughing. For the half an hour he couldn't find anything around. She was unable to tolerate the pain.

Without taking much time he decided to take her on his scooter. Her in-laws didn't find this as a good idea but under such circumstances there was no option in front of them and they have to comply with it.

She wore a sweater over her suit and a rain coat, covered herself from top to bottom; with gloves in her hand and high boots down.

They reached the city hospital within 10 minutes. The rain coat hasn't helped her nor had the nature. She was wet; soon hospitalized and the doctor recorded a high fever.

Heavy rains were supposed to change things.

"This could be fatal for any one of them. But don't worry we'll try our best" the doctor informed and left.

These words were a thunderclap for him. He didn't tell this to anyone. Not even her thinking she would lose all her strength.

She was under observation throughout the night. The nurse would come and check her every 30 minutes. He would run here and there for medicines, injections and completing other formalities. No doubt the situation was tight.

He was there with her the whole night praying all by himself. He wished everything gets normal soon. Although the whole night she cried in pain but nothing happened.

The rains had stopped before dawn and by morning the temperature was normal.

When the clock was about to touch twelve she delivered and heard a cry. This meant that everything was fine, she smiled.

It was just a start of many cries and a moment to be cherished by any mother in the world. It is an apex moment because it's the only time in your life when you cry and your mother smiles.

It was a sigh of relief for him. He informed the good news to his parents.

And so began the story of my life. Nine months she endured the pain and he stood for me. How they could have let me die even before seeing me.

In no time relatives and phone calls flooded in for greetings on the birth of first grandson of family.

After a glance at me everyone would say "Maa pr gya h!" They referred to my colour as my mom says.

Motherhood is a new chapter in any woman's life. It is something that helps her learn every day and she couldn't find an alternative substitute for that. She doesn't know what the future would unfold for her.

The first year of motherhood is a mixed bag - of celebrations, of joys, of sorrows, of sacrifices, of compromises, of laughs, of tears, of challenges, of changes, of everyday trials, of mental strength, of self-will, of determination, and of multiple assessments on the pinnacles of her energy, patience, love, priorities, values and selflessness.

I started catching words from others lips. Though couldn't make out but had some meaningless sounds out of the mouth.

"MAA" I called out for her. It was quite plain. After eight months I spoke my first word. Nobody heard that except her.

She felt that deeply, it was music to her ears. It had transported her to a different world; it was from her boy and for her.

After everyone knew about my first word out of the mouth, they would come to me and provoke me to say their name - Papa bol papa, chachu bol.

The beginning of my life was quite simple. I conquered love of all as the first child always does.

Every night after the dinner my uncle would take me in his lap for a night walk. I would never miss a chance of buying a small packet of Parle-G from the nearby store.

I hated people coming and picking me up as my mom told me. They would chub my cheeks and kiss me every time. I too was no less. I would pee on them. They would then hate me like I hated them.

20 days before my birthday I took my first step. I slipped out of my grandma's lap when I ran to chase the lizard on the wall. I took five steps and fell. They told me I used to call lizards 'kili'.

On my first birthday I used a walker. That was my first gift and that too from my grandparents.

The interesting part was my surprise birthday party. My parents too were not aware of it.

My parents had gone somewhere (I don't remember now) and I was asleep at home. It was in the late evening when my family people came early from work.

This birthday party was preplanned. It is when they reached home they got to know about it. They were dazed to see acquaintances.

Nothing until I got up; my mother dressed me in new clothes. I walked; I could see nothing but darkness. Scared; I held her hand firmly.

All of a sudden people in the hall started singing happy birthday song and the lights were on. I didn't understand anything but felt this sudden excitement and was over joyed to see the crowd. As usual they again picked me up and kissed my red cheeks.

In My Eternity

I had cut the cake with my mom and dad and messed up with my new dress.

They had gifts for me. One by one they came kissed and handed over the gift.

The party was finished but I was not. I had the eager to open up my gifts. They covered half of my bed and on the other half I and my father unpacked them. There was a dress, a toy train, a slate board with chalk, a Barbie doll set and a teddy bear.

Within a month after my birthday I had learnt how to walk without any support and could speak common words.

Chapter 2

Stepping Stone

Like most of the children in this world I too was made familiar with the temple of learning; I was admitted in school and that was the best turn of my life.

My first school 'Little soldier', a play school where I started in the year 2000.

We all experience two best days of the school life, 'The first' and 'The last' day of the school. Usually people don't remember their first day but surprisingly the last day of school life haunts many of us till the doom. And it's amongst the most beautiful days we would ever live and once in our lives; it's the source of never ending old memories of school.

Okay! I too remember my first day at school.

On the way to school my mother tenderly held my hand and looked at me fondly. The new road to the school seemed quite interesting to me. In the path I saw children of my age, in new clothes like mine, were timidly accompanied by their parents at school.

A strange and inexplicable feeling bloomed in my heart. Then I had a bit of fear when I caught sight of the elementary school. It looked so splendid.

In My Eternity

I held her hand firmly. She accompanied me to the school and to the classroom too. After every one had come, they took us in the main porch and made us stand in multiple rows. Command was given and everybody started singing.

I could see, like me none of them was involved in singing except the teachers and my mom too. Some children left it and ran towards their mothers.

I stood there with the remaining ones.

We went back where we were made to sit at first. My mother sat on a chair at the backside of the class taking care of a child who was to come in this world yet.

I watched her stomach grow with each passing month. My mother was becoming fat day by day. Had she being eating a lot?

No! there was my younger sibling inside.

At home, my uncle and aunts would bring toys in pairs. I see my grandma knitting small sweaters and things like my small bed in which I used to sleep, and others were slowly coming down from the loft in our room.

I was surprised to hear that my parents were going to have another child.

On the first day of the school, we didn't have any lessons rather they called up every child in the centre along with his or her mother for a brief introduction. I would turn back a hundred times in a minute to see whether she was there or not.

My mom accompanied me to the class for another day and on the third day she left me from the school gate.

How badly I wanted to cry for my mom but I knew she will come back and take me.

But that day she didn't. My father came and took me to the hospital.

I became an elder brother.

My mom gave the best gift to my father. It was a boy.

Now my brother and father had two consecutive birthday dates and when you add two more days to his birthday it would be my mom's birthday.

We four had a 'J' factor. My rest of the family was born in June and I in January. My parents married in July.

I remember one day, on a sarcastic note my father had said us that "you both have to maintain this custom. So you both should marry either in January, June or July."

As the days went on I developed a liking for the school. The teachers would make all of us all sing poems, "Johnny-Johnny yes papa" and "twinkle-twinkle little star" was much loved by me. We all would sing and act together and it was so much fun. The best part of play school was you need not carry a bag and all of the time, you just got to play.

My early days went well. Those were days for my social and emotional development. Those were my days of learning. Every day I used to hear a new moral story from my grandma. She would also teach me the Hindi alphabets- क ख ग. . ..! She read to me, wandering with me into the stories and the poems she thinks that I should know and understand.

A story fascinates me a lot since the day she had told me. It is a story, a genuine one.

In My Eternity

The British had stolen our wealth and culture, as she said. In 1947 when India got its Independence, there was massive carnage in the north-west part of the country. Indians who resided in Pakistan were forced to leave their home land. There was firing and mass killing to eradicate the Indians from their place. My great Grandfather and Grandfather were both a part of the astonishing tale. My Grandfather was born in Sindh, Pakistan in those days when India was on the verge of getting back its land from the British.

When the time came to leave the grounds they ran for their life. He was just eight years old back then along with his two other siblings. His elder sister got her left leg cut during the dark time. They had left behind all the property and money worth 50000, and only managed to bring Rs. 72 to India. My family was not the only one impacted but lacs and lacs of Hindus and Sikhs had faced the debacle. They moved to a nearby village in Amritsar but could hardly manage their daily bread for the next few years or so. Looking for work and comfortable place they moved to Indore.

Every week papa would buy a new story book for me; I hated toys. I would throw them instead of playing with them. I was busy in my own world with characters from stories, I longed to become like one of them.

I spent a complete one year at school. I had learned all the 26 alphabets in the English language, counting from 1-20 and know how to make a standing and sleeping line; that was the best and the easiest part with a pencil in your hand those days.

My mom told me that I used to cry because we didn't have school on Sundays. And so she had to sit with me on a Sunday morning and help me with reciting alphabets, numbers and working with lines.

I wished this was all I had to study till the end.

. . .

I see children playing on the slides; some were busy making their dream castles in sand. All of them were in the same dress.

We entered the main porch and were made to sit on steal chairs.

My mom took out a comb from her purse and combed my hair and then she looked at herself in the mirror.

There, maids offered us water and we were asked to sit for a while.

I didn't have the faintest of idea about what was going on?

Shortly we were called in the cabin and my parents were offered a seat. I sat on my mom's lap.

In front of us there were two women, and a man with Harry Potter spectacles.

The gentleman with rimmed spectacles had put forward a question to me. "What is your name, little boy?"

I hesitated in speaking but then I never spoke. I moved around and trying to hide my face and hugged mummy.

He meanwhile talked to my father when my mom took me outside the cabin. She wiped off my tears with her handkerchief.

"I'll buy you Chocolates and a Teddy bear if you answer the questions inside". The bait was set. She showed sharp daring eyes at me and took me inside.

In My Eternity

She apologised at first and then sat.

He didn't question me now.

One ma'am who was sitting at the right end asked me to sing my poem. At the drop of a hat I sang 'Johnny-Johnny' and 'Twinkle Twinkle Little Star'.

Next, they gave me a jigsaw puzzle to solve and identify the animal made.

I solved it before the given time and my acid test was over.

They interviewed my parents for the next couple of minutes and we went home.

My mother kept the promise she had made to me outside the cabin.

Two days later my father came home in between the working hours with a box of sweets in his hand.

He came to me, removed the rubber band and opened the box. He held the laddoo in my mouth.

I didn't know what that for was but if that was a Laddoo then there was no reason to ask for it.

"Ujjawal has cleared the admission test" he said that in a high note to my mother and popped a Laddoo in her mouth too.

This was the first time when I had made my parents and family proud. Sri Sathya Sai Vidya Vihar was amongst the high class institutions of Indore.

My mom strutted around as proud as a peacock after my admission. It was not easy to clear the entrance of such a highly reputed school. Anyone who came to the house was told about the news first, and then was asked for water.

I always looked for the answer to the question that why I was not invited or was there in my parent's marriage while I was there in my Uncle's? I never knew when people in my house got married. It was when I learned to understand things when my mother would make me sit in front of the television with her Marriage Cassettes playing.

I would every time cheer when I see people from my home on the screen. But then after I cried that why I was not there, I would ask it from my father, mother, grandparents, uncle and aunts. The answers were different from everybody.

When I got bored from this I shifted onto Cartoons.

It's a rare thing that makes a child change its habit by means of cartoons, perhaps the only luxury that childhood provided without any compromises. Somewhere you might never know how they changed you how they developed you and that somewhere you were a cartoon yourself in your times.

It was difficult for my mom to take my eyes off them. Couple of hours after school my eyes were fixed. Even though there was no new episode, I would watch the repeat telecasts day in and day out. I got invested in the characters and enjoyed the show.

Let's start with the name, 'Tom and Jerry'; my pair with Krishh was called by its name. I was Tom and he was Jerry. Soon after we got up from the bed I and he would go after each other messing up things in the house. Quite painful it seems to me but he won all the arguments because he was younger and my parents took his side. He would end up crying and I with a scolding.

'Popeye', until I had not watched it, I disliked spinach. He made me like it. I ate spinach hoping someday I will get same power like him.

Bob the Builder developed the creativity in me. In the area around the house when something was under construction, I'd enjoyed myself making wonders with sand. Digging holes into sand heap and making ways was too much fun then.

I am sure nobody would forget about 'Beyblades'. I remember one's Shantanu made me watch this cartoon and then showed his new toy (Beyblade). He had the one which conquered the others every time. I bought that and made my classmate purchase it too. I had developed a good Beyblade fever back in the school days and would take on fights with them in the recess. I updated myself with the new episodes so that I can have a good watch on which Beyblade was the strongest and then asked my dad to buy me. A will to win increased with every Beyblade fight.

I longed a Pikachhu travelling over my shoulders. I collected Pokèmon cards and exchanged it with WWE ones. And then there were Dexter, Courage the Cowardly Dog, Powerpuff Girls, Noddy, Oswald.

And Childhood was another life when the only tension was to have better and more cards than your friends, fight with your parents over silly cartoons, keeping an eye on the watch (even when you don't know how to see it) so that you don't miss a single episode, not listening to anybody, missing food because cartoons was the only drug filling your tummy in those days.

In between all such things, I grew up too fast. Childhood was the best season of all.

Chapter 3

An Inquisitive Teen

My mother and I drove to the hospital in silence. I walked into the room to meet my newly born brother. It was my Uncle and Aunt's third child.

Later, when I was a year and half old, they had a boy. Unfortunately, his story is altogether different from the rest of us.

The Doctor's mistake has cost them a life. She didn't operate well at the time of delivery. She cried with pain. For 12 hours, the baby was stuck on the edge, she couldn't push it out. It was hard for her; she had already lost all her strength in the beginning. It seemed the child was lost but her care and love hadn't let him die. The doctors had reported a malfunction in his mind which was caused within 12 hours of his birth. His nerves were blocked. It had a disturbing and a prolonged effect on him. He had lost his understanding on how to speak and walk though his mental state was sound. He couldn't walk but crawl alone. Don't know how to speak but he talks with his emotions. People treat him as an object of pity and some stay aloof.

They had a girl after four years and now a baby boy. Finally they had a regular born baby.

In My Eternity

He had a soft body texture. I held him in my arms. I don't know how I loved someone so quickly. I felt absolutely nothing before walking into the room and then suddenly at once. He was mine.

Within two days he was brought home. I longed if he could talk to me and play with me. I had altogether a different affection with him.

I gave a name to him, 'Bhavya' It means grand or splendid. It was a pleasant name and everybody like it well.

Since the day she came to my house for Bhavya, I have been noticing that every evening she comes in her balcony while we play cricket, she comes with a novel in her hand, spectacles on and would sit on the armed chair and read or pretend to read it, I don't know.

Her name is Summer. She is a Christian. Her glance was like once in a blue moon. She would never come out of her house. The only time I could see her was on a Sunday morning when she goes to the church with her family.

She was two years younger than me. I hadn't talked to her in those years. All I knew was her name.

I had frequent eye contacts with her that day. I don't know why we both were looking at each other.

Now if she looks at me, she also watches my game. I need to be striking and must improve my game just because a girl is looking at me.

I hit the next ball hard; I knew it will go long but instead of watching where it lands- before or beyond the boundary, I looked at her whether she watched it or not. Unfortunately she did not. Her eyes were down in the book.

"Kitna lamba six tha dekha" I shouted.

My purpose was to draw her attention, I was being showy. She looked at me and me at her; she smiled looking at me. That made my day.

She went inside her house before we had completed our game. I looked again and again at her balcony to see her whether she was back, I was waiting for her to come and watch my game.

Does it concern me? No, not at all.

Later in the day, I checked my Facebook account. I hardly had any friend request, messages and notifications at Facebook.

But today I saw a friend request and a message.

She had texted- "Sorry if u felt weird of me staring at u but it was so strange, isn't it."

I replied "Hahaha yeah for a start".

Next day it rained heavenly in the afternoon. The street was all flooded with mud and water, so we could not play.

It was a complete boredom. There was nobody at home except my grandma. Mom and my brother had gone out. There was no power too and I was bored to death.

The sky was cleared after a good shower and with a bit of luck there was no sun. The environment was unpleasantly cold. I took my Mp3 and went upstairs to the terrace.

I sat on the platform. On purpose, I looked at her terrace.

In My Eternity

She was there.

Her loose wet hair falling down her face made her look like a million dollars. Her eyes were so beautiful, it had a different sparkle.

I was shy to start a conversation but I badly wanted to. It kept hanging in my mind whether I should nudge or not. I decided to let her come to me.

I showed myself busy; meanwhile I practiced some lines in my head for the first meeting. I waited for her voice to fall in my ear.

"Hi Ujjawal!"

"Hi" I nodded along side.

I helped her jump the wall that was standing in between us. And there she was on my side.

We started the conversation. Only she talked. Her eyes made me forgot all my lines. We shared our areas of interests.

Until dark we conversed.

I wanted this to happen every day. Every day we would meet and talk.

But unfortunately not every day was a good day. We met every week and talked almost every day on social media. She was becoming my good friend, or maybe more to that.

Chapter 4

Magic!

A blue summer sky with cotton Candy clouds and all you want in these hot days was a quick dip into the pool. Its summer and the memories were just waiting to happen, summer fun had already begun. My family and I recently had a taste of summer. We toured Gujarat in the May days.

The temperatures remained high during the afternoon and it was only after mid eve the temperatures would start to fall and you could sense the chilly winds whistle pass your skin here in Indore.

With summer vacations on I had nothing to do rather follow my daily summer routine. Wake up late-eat-TV-eat-computer-eat-play-eat-sleep. Days went quickly and it was all too boring with the summer assignments from school.

I wished if something was left to do this summer. Who knows?

My most vivid recollection of that summer is something which was magic to me.

I didn't know my best friend Shantanu would make it so interesting.

I got a call from him someday and he had asked me to come home quickly, and said he has something to show me. I didn't have an inch of idea what it could have been. I followed as he said.

I reached his place within a couple of minutes. "Hey! Dude what is it that is making you so excited about and you want to tell that thing to me?" I questioned.

He went to lock the door and shut the entire window. I waited until he came back. There was nobody at his home, his parents had gone to visit someone in the hospital and he told me that time they won't be back until eve.

Well now he told me to close my eyes. He then took me to the next room and helped me to sit on the chair. And then I heard quick clicks.

"Open it"

I founded myself in front of the computer screen.

Boom! What is this going on? I stood up from my chair a bit nervous and excited.

"This is called Sex" he said in a soft voice. Before this I had only heard of it in school but haven't bothered to know what it was and that today I came to know that it was this bullshit thing.

This thing was too funny, this made me laugh and giggle a bit.

Male thing into the female thing. It goes in like inside and then leaks. "Eeeks, Fevicol?" I said. He patted me on my head and gave a bad look.

It was kind of a rebel from my side but my body was enjoying it.

I had a lot to ask now (my doubts), usually I didn't raised any questions in the class after the chapter but this lesson that my friend had taught me it was a complete blot on my mind.

"Is this for luxury or what?" I asked.

"Dude this is how babies are born" he said.

"Our parents did this?"

"Obviously" he said.

I made a Poker face. It means I also have to do this. No I will not marry instead. I had made the decision then and there itself.

"We are fools thinking here that an angel would come and gift a child to our mother" he added. There he seemed heated, like he is going to fight with the society for teaching us wrong. His parents had narrated him this story, mine was different.

It took me some time to grasp the fact, actually a lot of time. I think it was absurd. He had dropped a bomb on me that day.

"Why can't you make up good things man, like about ghosts and stuff, why do you even think about gross things like putting things in other things? If you put in so much effort into batting and bowling you can be a star player in the team."

And, I think, for that second, even he doubted what he had told me.

I and Shantanu were having the times of our life. We had not watched it twice not thrice but four times and it was Shantanu's sixth. We had spent the whole evening watching it.

Later in the night when I and my brother were on the bed I asked him this question "Do you know how babies are born?"

"Mom has told this a plenty of time, don't you remember?" He said.

"I don't remember tell me once again" the curiosity grew even more. Although I was aware of both the genuine thing and the made stories from our parents but I wanted to hear that again.

He refused to but after when I insisted several times by disturbing his sleep he finally narrated me.

"What happens is first our mummy goes to the doctor right? Then the doctor gives a seed which no one knows whether it is going to be a boy or girl. Mummy has to take that seed with water and then drink a lot of water until she becomes fat because that means that the seed has nourished and baby is growing and then the mummy has to go to the hospital. The doctor will do the operation and a baby is born" he relaxed and turned his head on the opposite side.

"Haha fool you also are among the thousands of other fool in this world. Sex" he didn't hear my last line but heard what I said in the end.

He got up and switched on the lamp kept on the bed desk near him. "Sex! Did you just say sex huh?" He stood up like he had been hiding a truth about sex from me and that I had come to know about it. For long he stared at me without blinking his eyes like I had solved life's greatest mystery by giving him a word.

"I don't know what you are talking about. Sleep now it's too late." I decided not to explain him this notion but he started bullying me that he would go and ask mom and dad what's this sex?

I found myself in a revolting situation. How could I tell a boy who is in fifth class about this things? And secondly if I don't then surely I would be resting in peace the next morning.

"Gosh what should I do?" I murmured. "Tell me fast" he answered quickly.

"Okay wait. Promise you won't use this word after this night anywhere. Okay?"

"Okay" he promised.

"It is nothing but to have love without wearing clothes. I mean totally nude. And after that babies are born."

"Seriously. . . are you mad? You know what someone had made you a fool and you don't know about it" he giggled.

"Perhaps" for a point of time I thought that Shanu has hoodwinked me on this concept of having babies and what my parents have told me is the right thing. After all they never lie.

"Are you really confident about what you told me?" He remained in the conversation.

"How do I know man? I haven't done it yet. When I'll do it I'll tell you."

He gave a not so cool expression. "Don't ask or tell anyone about it, you'll get a big slap" I said when he went to switch off the lamp. He ignored me completely, switched off the lamp and slept.

Whatever it is, it was love at first sight. I discovered my first masturbation that night. Having it on my bed, I used to wait for my brother to fall asleep and I would think of good looking girls to get the feel.

In My Eternity

I had done it for a couple of weeks unless I discovered this sudden analogy, what if some naughty sperms crawl out of my underpants onto the bed and then get into a vagina gifting her babies out of nowhere. I had stopped doing it then.

There was no sense to my understanding when Shantanu gave answers to these and then I was regular getting my underpants wet every night. He was the only one in those days with whom I shared how much I stroked last night and he too.

This everyday relief gave me acne and pimples on my face, Shantanu had already warned me about it. Although, mom and dad thought that I was in my puberty stage, they were happy I was finally growing into a man.

Shantanu and I now had something apart from projects for the rest of the summer. Alternate days we would go to the cyber cafe and would take the last seat every time and would enjoy our chips and coke along with porn. We completed a long list of special variety like Spanish, Italian, Chinese, French, American porn. Although we tried Indian once but it didn't electrify us. Made in China was better than India.

Everyday we learned a new word from the web after our chapter.

Now we knew what sex actually was - There is magic to it. A 'feel' we as children can never reach.

Schools were on by the time and we both had our tight schedule. Sometimes he was free at times I was, but once in a week we would manage to the cyber cafe.

We would save more from our pocket money to see such films.

Was there any end to this madness? I asked myself. No it seems.

Summers have come to an end, Not the World exactly. Just the summer. There would be other summers, but never be one like this. EVER AGAIN.

Every summer has a story I also had one!

. . .

My father had bought me a new phone. For a start it was a basic Samsung phone. I was happy and sad at the same time. I was happy because I got my first phone and sad because it was just a basic model with not even a camera.

"Papa what is this? You should have bought a good piece" I argued on his choice.

"Look this is only for your emergency use. You go out, so for your safety I have bought this for you and I think there is no need for you to buy expensive mobile phones at this age" he said. I not argued further.

I saved contacts of friends and relatives in my phone. The contact number that I desperately wanted in my phonebook was of Summer's.

Damn how will I ask her?

Only ten days were left for the 8th class half yearly examination and I hadn't started preparing for it. It was time to pull my socks.

I prepared my time table for studying according to the exam time table. First paper was Hindi followed by English and I decided not to study these before because they were easy. Social Science had two days off and thus not a problem in that. I started with Science and Maths because these two subjects never got into my head.

I somehow managed to learn my answers by heart and revise it before bed time for all exams. I had attempted all the papers well.

But now it was the last paper and that too maths. Generally my excitement of the last paper was endless and this excitement didn't let me study. I had only one day to prepare for it.

Integers, Mensuration, geometry and Algebra were all out of my reach. I had a hard time with these topics. It would make my blood run cold. These were in the syllabus and not even a simple chapter. I was screwed.

I came home from school after my social science exam.

Without wasting much time I took lunch and started preparing for maths. I knew I had to combine day and night to understand and grasp maths.

I studied for relentless two hours until I had a headache. I wanted to go out and play to refresh my mind but I decided that music and terrace was the best things to get rid of a head ache.

This time I saw her again. I thought I should talk to her, it'll make me feel better and maybe she can serve as my stress buster.

I waved at her; she said a Hi and waved back.

The first question she had asked me that evening was "do you use a phone?"

"Yes, its been two months that my dad had bought me one."

"Idiot you should have asked for my number then. Leave now, give me yours."

How effortlessly she had asked me for my number which I was dying to exchange with her for two months?

We didn't talk much. She was upstairs for some work and she had done it already so now she went. I spent half-n-hour more listening songs and then went back to study.

I studied for one hour after that and then went out for dinner with my family. Still half of my syllabus was left.

When I reached home it was already midnight and I didn't yearn to study. I was tired and sleepy. But I had to complete my chapters somehow.

I sat again. After an hour into the books I got up to quench my thirst. In between I checked my phone.

I saw a text message from Summer. It was delivered 20 minutes ago when I checked it.

Summer: 'Hi! Are you free to talk?'

'Hey, why not?' I messaged her back.

I waited for her reply. But there was not a single beep on my phone for the next 10 minutes.

I heard the message notification after few minutes and ran for the phone like a dog runs for a bone. It was her message.

We messaged each other continuously. I studied in between the time I got when I waited for her message. To be honest while talking to her I was not concerned about my maths exam, there was Summer in my head.

We ended up texting at 3:10AM. We had exchanged over 150 text messages. To be on the safer side I deleted the messages before sleeping. I feared that anyone from the family does not come to know about me chatting with her last night.

Chapter 5

Debacles

"Children, keep quiet or else I won't show you your marks."

She was sitting right in front of me with those half yearly exams' answer sheets.

I already feared math. I had to struggle with each and every topic of it. I didn't know why? May be because I didn't pay enough attention or I was weak at it or may be the teacher doesn't teach well or simply I didn't study well. There could be hundreds of reasons why I cannot handle mathematics. But one reason was for sure, 'because it was math.'

She waited until the whole class was quiet.

"Okay, so everybody pay attention here! This time what we'll do is before handling you your answer sheet you have to get up and make a guess of how much you have scored? Is it all right? And whosoever guesses it accurately will get an addition of 1 mark." Everyone agreed and actually we had to.

Nobody in the class dared to talk against her views or ideas. It was like kicking yourself into the fire-well.

She started distributing answer sheets roll number wise. Nobody up till then had a correct guess. Four out of 36 had already failed and the lowest score was 11 out of 50. The topper till then was Yash with 44 marks.

I didn't know I was going to make history this time. It was my turn- the second last roll number in the class.

I stood up. She held her both eyebrows high. Her gestures showed that I haven't scored good marks. I knew I wouldn't score more. To be frank, I said "20". I slipped my tongue I wanted to say a bit less but my tongue respected my image in front of everybody in the class. Everyone stared at me in awe. Twenty was the border line that separated the failed from the rest.

She stood in despair.

"It's below your expectation and mine too. I am surprised by your performance, Ujjawal. Better luck next time! You have scored a sweet sixteen. Come here fast and take your copy." She said that in disregard.

I took my copy, felt ashamed; I was not able to have an eye to eye contact with her or anybody in the class. I went back to my place without responding to anyone.

I have failed for the first time in my life in any test. I couldn't blame anybody or anything. Had I not texted her the whole night before the math paper, things would have been different.

Tears fell down my cheek. In order to hide them, I sat with my head down. In those days, Ishan was my bench partner. He had also failed his math test.

The biggest problem was that all the students had to get the answer sheet signed by their parents and submit it by tomorrow.

At home I didn't tell anyone. I slept the whole day to get rid of that thought from my mind. I got up late in the evening. It was Monday and papa was home early. I avoided his company that day.

He called me inside his room and asked me about my marks.

I hesitated. I went into my room and took out the other answer sheets from the bag. I skipped math.

I showed him my marks. I have scored well in the entire exam and till now my average was 38 out of 50, excluding math. It was good enough. I got it signed from him.

"You haven't got your math marks huh?" he asked.

"Umm. . . the teacher is on a leave for two days so we have not yet got the marks, we are expected to get it day after tomorrow."

"Okay" he said and I left his room.

"What will I do in the school tomorrow? What will I answer her? It doesn't matter now. I have made an excuse here; I will handle it in the school also." I conferred myself.

Next day in the school Ishan had helped me escape the problem.

"Did you have the math answer sheet signed?" I asked Ishan.

"No" after a pause continued "I did it myself. I know my father's sign and I can copy it well" he replied.

"Listen? Can you help me, please? Copy my father's sign and do it on my maths answer sheet. Dude please!" I begged.

"Okay, show me how it goes first."

"See this." I showed him my father's sign on the other answer sheets.

In My Eternity

"It is convoluted bro, but I'll give it a try" he said.

I took out my rough notebook and handed him to practice on it.

He practiced it 10 times and on the 11th go he had done it accurately. I hope he doesn't make a mistake while he is signing the answer sheet. I gave him my new Parker Ball pen. "Do it" I said. It was risky. One mistake and I'll be fired from both the sides. It was terrifying. He also knew that the job wasn't easy.

"Don't worry, even if you make a mistake I'll take the blame on myself for doing this." I tried to relax him.

His hands shivered as he picked up the pen. Before he could touch the nib on the answer sheet and start to sign, I stopped him.

I took my pen. "Sign it with the pen from which you had practiced." I said.

I again hoped for the best as he picked up his pen. He moved his hands. I closed my eyes.

Nothing could be better than this. He had accurately copied my father's sign. There was a great relief. Now I had no tension, the greatest fear was set aside.

I thanked him for saving my life. Until the result day I had no burden on my head. By the day I get the report card I can make excuses about the math answer sheet at home. We didn't tell anyone in the class about what Ishan did.

Math had taught me well that yes everything has a solution even if it is the other way.

'Remember everything has a solution, may be you'll get it too early or too late but you'll get it. Nothing could be changed until you decide to face it'.

The problem was temporarily solved and there was lasting relief in me.

My father had forgotten about my math marks and I didn't care enough to inform him about the blunders I have done in my math paper.

After a week, we got our report card of the half-yearly examination. Math marks were like a blot on my sheet of paper. I could see 16 written with an E grade corresponding to Mathematics. The every time I saw that I cursed myself up for late night chat with Summer.

I had scored 46 in Sanskrit. Those were the highest marks in the class. But my heart was not proud of them but ashamed of those 16 marks. I founded myself in an ugly middle position. This time I had no option left. I had to show it to my parents. I went back home. Sad.

After dinner I went to my parent's room with my report card and showed it to them.

"Papa sorry I don't know how but. . ." I had not completed the whole sentence and tears fell down my eyes. He had seen it. I could sense that he was unhappy and my mother was burning like coal. She raised her hand to slap me but my father had stopped her on the right time. She was so angry and annoyed that she could have beaten me up.

"Listen, come here" he said.

I sat beside him. I thought maybe he had stopped her from slapping because he wanted to give me a tight one. I was scared. I couldn't stop crying.

"I already knew that you have failed in your math exam. Your teacher had already called me earlier and informed me. I am not disappointed because you failed; I am upset because you were not brave enough to let us know. I had not forgotten but I was waiting for you to come and tell me. And talking about the answer sheet; ma'am understood that it was a fake sign and knew that you must have imitated it. She immediately cross checked with me. I went to the school and signed your answer sheet. I said sorry to her and promised her that any such thing would never happen again, I'll take care of that." He paused for a moment. "Tell me one thing. Didn't you think about our self-respect while forging our signs? Are we fools here huh? Tell me the reason why you scored so less marks?" His tone changed after the respite.

I said nothing. I didn't have the guts to answer it. I never felt so much embarrassment and regret in my life in front of my parents.

He then instructed me to study math an hour every day. If I had doubts he had asked me to note it down and said he will clear them after he comes from work. He himself was a math champion and had scored twice full marks in the subject when he was in school.

He then said to me something that still haunts proudly in my mind. "Don't cry at your failure in first attempt. Remember even a successful math starts with a zero only"

Nobody in the class was aware of what had happened. I quietly went and apologized to her for whatever I had done.

I told Summer my whole story. She felt sad for it.

She apologized a lot. I was too responsible for it. I cursed myself for so many days but couldn't get out of the pain.

I was scared that I might not do anything silly or offending like that again and that would make my parents feel offended.

After what happened with me in the math exam I decided to stay away from girls. Actually she was the only girl in my life. I didn't reply to her messages on Facebook nor texted her on direct messages. We would meet by chance and talk.

But things couldn't make up for me. I started ignoring her.

She was upset about what was going on between us. She didn't like how I was behaving with her. She tried to make things good but I wasn't ready. She would talk with every one excluding me. I was jealous but I didn't care.

We were best friends one day but now we stayed aloof. Time flew, days passed and seasons changed but we were still the same.

On Deepawali, she came to me while I was burning crackers. After a long time we were standing in front of each other.

Her eyes were still the same. I stared at them. It looked thoughtful as if it had so much to say, so much to ask about. They were endlessly deep.

"Ujjawal, I waited for so long. But it doesn't matter now.

I found someone. I have a best boy friend now."

"I am happy for you" I said softly. Those lines were never true.

She meant a lot to me. I never wanted to walk away from her life but I had no other option in front of my eyes.

I showed up as if I didn't care because that caring would have made me weaker towards her. But I wanted to know who the boy was? Where he came from?

Later on I got to know from Harsh itself that he was dating her. He is my cousin. I then understood why he came every evening and joined us for cricket. She would come in her balcony like before but not for me but for him. Things were different now. I did not bother much because he was my brother and we had a good bonding between us. I didn't want anything between me and him because of Summer.

I didn't want to hurt her again so I quietly moved out of her days. That was the first time when I understood what maturity was.

We, under no circumstances talked with each other. There was kind of ego between us.

· · ·

Months passed after Bhavya's birth and we were expected to see his hand and leg movements. We took absolute care of him and had him all the vaccination required on time. But he was not ready for the movements nor would he roll here and there while sleeping. We didn't notice any kicking or stretching from him in the beginning of the two months. He didn't gain any weight either.

He rather started to lose health and turned weak. Maybe the mother feeding had not helped him regain his energy.

We soon consulted our family doctor for this. Even after his prescriptions we didn't see any changes.

We went to another doctor and had his blood test.

I woke up to an overcast sky. Heavy rains were expected shortly. The weather was cold and pleasant. The nature looked fresh.

Heavy rains are unlucky for me. I have an illogical fear to it. Looking at the dark clouds it seems that the whole world has lost its happiness. It seems to me that nothing good and profound is left on the earth. All filled with negative energy. On the other hand, rains also meant a disheartening news for me most of the time. I feel uncomfortable when it rains and so to avoid it, I sleep.

Today was a holiday in school. My school used to have it off on the second Saturday of the month.

There was drizzling first followed by heavy rains. The water hit the ground fast with thicker water droplets. There was continuous lightning. It made my fear grew larger.

As always I just hoped and wished that I didn't get a bad news today. I took my lunch and to avoid the frustration from rains I slept again.

I had slept on the couch itself in the living room. I got up late in the evening when I heard cries. I could see my grandma was crying and my uncle too had watery eyes.

I left the living room and walked straight to my room without saying a word. I was afraid. I knew something was wrong. I wanted to know what.

After sometime my mom came into my bed room with supper. I could see her face was dull too.

"Mom, what happened?" I asked. My brother stood inquisitive.

She didn't want to answer my question but I compelled her to do so.

"Today chacha went to the doctor to collect Bhavya's report. The doctor said he is suffering from Thalassemia." I echoed, blankly. I had never heard of the disease before.

"Oh! And what is that?" I questioned, sipping my juice.

"It is a form of blood disorder in which there is no formation of haemoglobin. It further leads to malfunctioning of the body in different ways. There is insufficient oxygen transport in the body. And every month we need to change the blood" she said.

"So can't we change his blood every time?" I further inquired dumbly.

"That's not the only thing Ujjawal. Understand the situation. The worst part of the sickness is that he can die any moment. And we don't have any treatment to this. He has Thalassemia Major." I was taken aback at her sentence. I couldn't gulp the food in my mouth. It just couldn't move down my throat.

There was great despair among the family members that day. My uncle's second boy was also deviated.

How must have they felt of not having the pleasure of a boy.

'Karma, as you say will give you things only according to how you acted before. Also remember that things revert. Let Karma settle it.' They cursed Karma for the whole situation.

They decided to have the tests again; may be the reports prove wrong this time.

For a few days we waited for the second reports. But before it gets serious, we took him to the hospital to alter his blood.

Within a week came the reports. It was our hard-luck. The reports were same as earlier. There was not a slight change in it.

The disease had come mysteriously.

Chapter 6

The Void

I got up for school in the morning. I bathed and got down to take my breakfast.

I heard voices coming from the corner of the room while I was having my sandwich. It was my grandfather who was speaking with the family people about some distribution of property.

We the children were taking our breakfast in the drawing room just then he called us inside his room and asked us to sit near him. We all the 15 family members stood in his room; all the children including me on his bed.

He had not got up from his bed from the past 6 months. He was suffering from lung cancer. Everyone was aware in the family that he is our few days guest now. When I came to know that he was diagnosed with cancer I felt like I needed to be with him. So I fetched some time for him from my day.

He started with me since I was his eldest grandson. He put a hand over my head and said "Ujjawal take care of each and every one in the family. Be a good child. Always find a good company to be with. Don't get involve in bad stuffs ever and listen the first income that you are going to get use some part of it to buy food and give it to the beggars and poor people in front of any temple".

I don't know why he said those words but I quietly kept listening.

After me he called one younger than me. I heard my auto rickshaw horn and it was my time to leave. As usual I touched his feet like every day I did before leaving for school. He smiled at me elegantly.

Throughout my school I thought why he had suddenly gathered all the family members and why he was talking about such things. He had told me all these things earlier also but today why and that too in the morning? But something unusual is going to happen; my mind said.

Ma'am was teaching us the rules of participles. Just then the school peon interrupted her. He came up with a slip. Ma'am called out my name when she had finished reading it.

"Ujjawal your father has come to take you. Take this slip."

'What could be the possible reason that dad had come school to pick me up from school and that too early?' I took the slip from her. I read it.

There it was mention in the reason 'Grandfather Expired' and at the bottom I could see my father's signature.

It was like a slap on my face. I didn't say anything to anyone; packed my bag and quietly left the classroom. In between I went to the staff-room to inform my class teacher about my half-day at school.

I saw my father from a distance. He looked pale and sad. I confronted him and he narrated what had happened.

In My Eternity

I saw my younger brother on the scooter. Papa had picked him up from school before me. He had tears in his eyes. But there was something that didn't made me cry.

As we drove towards our house some happy moments flashed through my mind with him. I understood why he assembled all of us in the morning. Perhaps he came to know his time has come.

I remembered the time when he had gifted me a new computer, whenever I wanted money I would go and ask him for that. He was our children's Bank with unlimited cash balance in our accounts. I could recall that moment when I was a kid I use to stand and walk on his back and help him get rid of the back pain he used to felt after work. I thought of him resting on the chair in the veranda laughing with me.

I hadn't really thought I won't see him again after this morning. I thought he would always be there. I wasn't prepared for what had happened. I didn't know those would be his last words.

The last smile of his was the most beautiful of all.

We reached home. I saw many vehicles parked in and around my house and people standing in front of the house. I went upstairs in the drawing room where my grandfather lay. I heard ladies crying and mourning.

My Grandfather lay in his traditional button down white kurta covered with a shroud in one corner of the drawing room. He had his eyes shut tightly. He was stopped forever now.

My grandma was sitting near the dead body. She looked like a late winter's moon.

She called me near her. I bent forward to her. She embraced me and cried on my shoulders.

I didn't know how to react in such situation? I didn't know what to do? I remained quiet.

I changed from my school uniform to a casual dress. I sat quietly with my little cousins in the room.

We were all called for his final appearance in the house.

Up till now I had not shed a tear out of my eyes. But when it was his final moment I started crying. I cried only for a point of time but I cried badly.

I saw Summer looking at me through her balcony. I felt ashamed. I tried to hide myself from her in the crowd.

We offered 'Ardas' as the final prayers.

Seeing him lie all stood gazing at him in mute numbness. They picked him up to leave him to the holly gates. I was too small to give him my shoulders but then my father had asked me to do it. They bent it a little for me and my younger brother. It lay heavy.

Countless number of men was in the parade, speaking in unison to pay respect to the man. I too repeated with them. We bid him adieu by tossing flowers over his motionless body.

For the first time I visited the richest place in the world; Graveyard. I had learned from somebody that spirits haunt the place.

I was scared.

I racked with pain when he gave fire to the dead body. I quietly stood in the corner watching him mix in the five elements of the earth. His world was converted into a single grey ash thing.

We all men came home. The day was completely unlike than the other days. First time in my life I had experienced such a debacle. It was one of the greatest setbacks in my life.

A few days later, the time to hold a mass in honour of my departed grandfather came. My family members, neighbors, and family friends met in local Gurudwara where several family speakers gave speeches about the good quality times they could recall with him.

A week after he passed away I was back to my daily routine. Things seemed really changed when one family member was not there. His permanent seat at the dining table was taken over by Bhavya when he had learned to sit.

The two seats at the dining table were empty that day. Papa had already informed about their late meeting with the client and thus they won't be able to make it at home on time.

As soon I got up from the dining table papa came home. He looked happy that time. There was a different spark on his face. It showed as if he had clinched a big order or something from the client.

Nobody had finished dinner yet except me. Bhavya was struggling with his one chapatti from the past 15 minutes. Chachu approached him and picked him up.

"Bhavya ab tu theek ho jayega. Ab koi injection nahi lagega aur doctor k yaha nahi jaana padega" he said and kissed him. Bhavya didn't understand anything rather he just kept looking at him from the moment he said the word injection.

Bhavya was scared of the needle and the every new person he met. He had developed Anthrop phobia. He thought every new person he would meet he or she will chase him and give him an injection.

There was a sudden ecstasy at the dining table. I jumped for joy.

He responded two years late but had heard our prayers.

Daadi couldn't believe what he just told us and not even I. Everyone left their food and was keen to know except Bhavya how his Thallasemia can be cured? He dragged an empty seat and sat near his wife. I and my father remained standing.

"Hira Lal ji met me during papa's demise. After I told him about Bhavya he asked me to approach his acquaintance whose only child is also suffering from Thallasemia. So today after work Kamal and I went to their residence to enquire about him. Unfortunately we had not met him (the child). He was somewhere out with his friends.

But we learned from his parents that he is 20 years old now and after every 10 days he needs to change his blood. They had also mentioned that this disease is curable and because they were not aware of its remedy they were not able get his operation done. Only children below five years of age can get out of this."

"It costs 25lacs for the operation" my father cut him. He had lost his promising smile there.

It was not in our reach. I was well aware of the harsh realities that my family was going through. I could sense and understand their emotions very well. Gathering 25lacs was not going to be an easy task for us. We had to give in everything that we could.

"25 lacs is just the operation cost. It would add 2-3 lacs of accommodation more" he added.

There was a not understanding silence in the hall. Nobody said anything. Everyone remained quiet until Bhavya interrupted the silence by cheering "main first a gya maine chapatti finish kr di" and then he clapped all for himself.

It is silly how Bhavya does not understand his own situation. His body feels the pain of syringes every month. He is not able to put that pain and suffering in words. He sees many children like him lying on the bed kept adjacent to his bed in the hospital and live with an understanding that every child has to go under such kind of things. We tell him not worry that it is a matter of few days and that we also had the same thing when we were young. He thinks upon it for a time and then forgets it.

He lives in a happy world which is his own. He always finds happiness in small-small things, always trusts with his eyes closed, always hopes, and keeps no records of wrong.

He taught me how to love the ordinary. That there are really places in our heart that we didn't even know they exist until we love a child because that is something you could learn the best from them.

What screws up me most is his condition, how it ought to be.

My father and uncle both were determined to take him to Delhi so he took the appointment from the doctor in the next week.

It seemed like a ray of hope but a start never the less.

I had a message from Summer the day when Dada Ji passed away. I checked it after a couple of weeks.

'Ujjawal please don't cry. I can't see you crying. I have so much to say you right here. First thing is that I Love You. Second what all I have done in the past days was all a fake. I don't love him a bloody inch. I am not in love with Harsh. I dated him only because I wanted to make you jealous. I wanted to draw your attention towards you. But I think that never affected you.

I wanted to tell you that after the finals i.e. in march I'll be shifting to Pune permanently my father is having a transfer there. Please lets be friends again like we were before? Let's not fight anymore while I am still here. I beg you. I miss my friend and I want him back. These four months are all I have. I'm going to miss being able to jump the fence and meeting you. I am going to miss those accidental glances which make my heart skip a beat. I'm going to miss all of this, all of you. Please forgive me.

Give me back my best friend.

I was struck dumb when I read that message. 'She loves me?'

'See Summer If you ask me I was jealous too. Every day that part killed me. Don't ask me why I treated you that cold, actually I had no intensions for that. I was tired of getting my hopes up when it comes to you, so I quit trying and expecting. I wish I would have not done that. And now you'll be leaving in a few months and I am going to miss you. Forget everything, come to me and yes common let us make these four months the best'.

Chapter 7

Last Days of Summer

It was time when Summer and her family members started with their packing. She was about to leave within a week. My liking for her increased more as the date approached nearer. I had decided that I won't allow this thing to happen again. Throughout the exams I kept my phone switched off. But I didn't keep myself away from her.

My 10th class final exams concluded 2 days before she was going to leave. As usual we all started with cricket in the evening. His younger brother would also play with us.

The day after my exam I saw her at her terrace while I was playing cricket. I wished I could make an excuse with my mates and run up to my terrace and have a last time with her at the terrace. I wanted to end things up the way they were started.

The terrace was the best part of our story.

I couldn't find any excuse for the half n hour of the play. After sometime I saw her parents and grandparents leaving for church as it was a Sunday. They had taken her brother along with them. Summer was all alone at home.

I again and again looked up for her. She signalled me to come up. It gave butterflies in my stomachs.

'I had to go now no matter what. This could be our last meeting alone. Common find a way Ujjawal?

I unnecessarily postponed her. Told her from my emotions that I am coming, but I was blank. How do I get to her?

If I tell these kids they would start to make fun of me and God Shantanu would kill me for it if I go alone just to meet her.

I wanted only five minutes pause from the game. And secondly didn't want Shantanu to accompany with me.

I played more and thought more. The worst rule of our game was that whosoever hits the ball in any house of the street has to fight for it and get it back from the auntie.

But it somehow clicked my mind that this rule can help me to meet her.

I was ready to cost my wicket for her.

From the next ball I tried hitting hard and towards the roof top of her house. At first I stroked it well that it cleared the boundary. She applauded for it.

Second time I had missed the ball completely.

The third time I succeeded. Though it was intentional but the way I played it, it didn't look fake.

I showed them how disheartened I was as I failed to take my team to victory.

Now as per the rule I went upstairs to take the ball. A feeling of elation ran through my arteries. My heart pumped love instead of blood.

In My Eternity

I saw her on the terrace but damn she was talking to my mom. Mom had taken my place which I desperately wanted at that time.

'Why now? Mom go please.' Mom noticed me as I came. So I had to talk to her.

"Mummy ball dekhi kya" I interrupted them.

She turned back and gave me a smile.

I went near her and stood there. I know the ball was on Summer's terrace but then too I asked mom to look for it on our terrace.

She said nothing and separated us.

I told Summer to meet me at the staircase. I showed myself busy in front of mom by looking for the ball though I knew where it was. My friends were shouting from downstairs and then there was mummy. I had problems from all the corners of the earth.

I found the ball and showed her so that she would stop searching for it. Although to my friends downstairs I had said that I am still searching for it.

"Shall I come up and help you" Shantanu shouted.

"No no I'll do it myself. No need buddy" I hesitated while I spoke. I stole eyes from him.

I quickly went to the staircase where she was waiting for me to come.

I stood in front of her. "Summer I haven't told you this in front of you but I know we had hundred times told each other on messages. I Love you bitch. I am going to miss you and everything. Try missing me."

"Stupid. I love you to the moon and back. Never leave my life please. Always be the best friend and I am also going to miss you and all that we had between us" she said.

She wanted to say something else also but my brother stopped her from doing so. He shouted "Did you find it?" "Yes I have got it. I am coming" I said.

We both stood staring at each other. As if she was waiting for me to do something. There was absolute silence between us. All I could hear was the chirping of the bird.

I just wanted a hug. A tight hug that could make me feel happy and that would add another memory and bliss to our story.

She came near me. I took a step forward. We were now just 3 inches away from each other.

I looked at her glossy pink lipstick. She had fortunately mistaken what my eyes were asking for?

What happened next was completely unexpected from my side.

She went for my lips. I didn't stop myself and leaned forward. I raised my hands towards her waist and grabbed her tightly in my arms. I could feel her breast on my chest. I could feel her soft hands around my neck.

We kissed in a hopeless place.

It came in the middle of the sentence that mine and her eyes were having. We had exchanged kisses a thousand times between our eyes before but today we actually went for the lips. It was that kind of kiss that made me know that I was never to happy in my whole life.

I sucked her lipstick. It tasted good.

The only thing that was missing was background music. It would have made it sensational. I had already watched these things happening in Hollywood movies but freak, it happened with me.

Finally we stopped. It went long but seemed it lasted for a second. I didn't want to stop. I wanted more of it. We both smiled looking at each other after it ended.

"Christians main sab chaltae" She said.

I chuckled.

My arms were still around her back. We kissed again but it was a French kiss this time.

Next I did what I wanted to. I hugged her tight and kissed her cheek.

The whole night I thought about what happened and what more could have happened between us.

Next day in the morning I got up late at 12 noon and went with my cup of coffee in the balcony. I saw a huge truck almost blocking the road in front of Summer's house. I could see some workers loading things. I saw a refrigerator, a bed, a study table and several things perfectly arranged in the truck.

Still there were 5 hours left for her flight. She had already informed me that they will be leaving from here at 2:30 for the airport.

15 minutes before 2:30 I heard Summer shouting my name. I went out to the balcony and saw many aunties on the road. They had come to bid farewell to her family. I looked for her and found she was standing right in front of my house. She called me down.

I didn't want to go because her father was also there in the crowd. Her father and I didn't have a good bonding. He hated me for being Summer's friend. Every time he saw her daughter with me he would call her back home with no reason. But he didn't have any problem with Shantanu. Her dad had previously warned me to keep away from her. May be that was the reason we didn't get into a relationship afterwards.

Summer was too aware of it but we both didn't cared.

I asked my family members to go downstairs and meet them as they are leaving.

My mom, grandma and chachi went downstairs to bid them farewell. I decided to remain upstairs in the balcony.

She requested me to come downstairs a 100 times. But I was stern I didn't go. I was scared of her dad.

Now when everybody was done, his father instructed their car driver to start the engines.

She went inside at last for the window seat. She winked at me before she opened the car gate.

"Yeh nahi sudhregi. Pagal!" I said and smiled.

The car flew away.

2 years of friendship with her gave me everything. I realised that now there would be no more stealing glances, no more

romantic meetings at the terrace. I will miss everything like hell.

After few days I told Shantanu about our accidental kiss. He was amused to listen what happened and why I took so much time on the terrace.

I requested him to do not cross check it with her as in she'll feel embarrassed.

. . .

My uncle and aunt arrived home two days late from Delhi. The doctor had delayed their appointment.

That day at the dining table while having dinner he discussed what happened in Delhi.

"The Doctor took several tests of his blood and DNA. He also took my sample. He handed over the reports within an hour. The reports were positive i.e. he is anytime ready for the operation. It is nothing but a bone marrow transplant. The Doctors would take DNA from Yash and would transplant it in Bhavya. This transplant will give a new birth to Bhavya. For two months we would need to keep him safe. A single bit of the mosquito can cause problem. If he falls ill or gets an infection within that period then even the Doctors cannot do anything and there is no chance of operating again. It is a one time operation. It will be severe. Chances are low too. I discussed about the cost with the Doctor and he said it is not going to be above 20lacs.

The Doctors have called us for the operation in the next year. But before this we need to inform him before Diwali that if we are ready or not because there are some recovery cells which needs to be brought from Germany and it would take time" He said.

"Inform the Doctor that we are ready for the operation." He put hand over my cha-cha's shoulder and said "Don't worry about the money. We'll find a way" giving him confidence.

You know that is something best about a good relation. The elder brother always looks up to his younger one. There is unconditional love and eagerness to sacrifice things for others. A sense of understanding the problems of our own family members and giving them hope that everything would be fine one day.

"The Doctor has given contacts of few families who got the operation done. Out of these only 4 were successful."

"What if he doesn't recover after the operation and the infection still remains?" I was being unoptimistic and I don't know why. Out of curiosity I asked it.

He took time to reply as if he was buried in some thoughts.

"Nothing the situation would be like before."

"Eh we are spending so much amount and then too such a downside."

Nobody spoke on the dining table after that. Every one took their food in utter silence.

At bed time when everybody was in their room my father approached us.

"Both of you listen carefully. I don't want you both to waste money now. We need a huge amount for Bhavya's operation and we need to start saving funds from now. I am sorry to say that this year no new phones, no school trips, and no branded things. Buy things only if there is an emergency unless otherwise it's okay not to buy it. We'll buy it some other time. Okay?"

I don't know why he said sorry. Doesn't he know that we are now mature enough to understand the situation?

I just wished my dad would find some money for his operation and things get straight with the little boy.

Chapter 8

The Twists and Turns of Life

"My mom came into my room yesterday. She came in with this white colour sheet in her hand. I ignored her as I was busy arranging my cupboard. I saw her through the mirror she was removing my paperwork from the pin board which was just above the study table.

I left my cupboard as it is and approached her.

"What are you doing maa?"

She said nothing until she made up some space for the sheet.

She picked up the sheet and while opening it she said "I am pinning these rules over here. It would be better if you follow these or else I'll make more of them and stricter ones"

I read them. You won't believe what was written on it.

Rules

1. STAY AWAY FROM GIRLS.
2. NO PARTIES THIS YEAR.
3. DON'T GET INVOLVE IN BAD STUFFS.
4. SUBMIT YOUR PHONE AT 11'O CLOCK TO ME.
5. PLAY LESS OF FIFA!

READ THIS 5 TIMES IN A DAY:

'I WILL SCORE 100% IN CLASS 12TH'

Ab bta main ki kra? I used my Punjabi accent.

Raj giggled when I told him this. "Bhai teri mummy ne to teri lga di" he continued laughing. "Haa yr ye to galat h" I sighed. The time came when we started counting our few months in the school.

In school Raj poisoned my ears and made me jealous regarding the whole thing. I decided to fight with her for it when I reach home.

"What rubbish is this? Nobody does these kinds of things with her child. Why are you so rude to me?"

She said nothing and left the room. I shouted at her back "Listen I am not going to do all these things. Do you understand?"

Since it was my 12th my mom wanted me to adhere to these rules strictly. She wanted me to get a good heavy percentage in class 12th.

I read those lines again and again. It frustrated me whenever I looked at the pin board.

I really thought about my rules. What can I follow? Rule one was okay. Since I had controlled on girls, but why no parties? It's the only time I could dance and enjoy with my friends. The third rule is fine, I never drink nor do I have any bad habits. I would never follow the fourth rule as I would never give my cell phone to her.

It was the fifth rule that broke me totally from inside. How can I live without my love? FIFA is everything for me.

I am not going to follow this, I confirmed myself.

As I moved down my eyes on the sheet I saw 'With Love Maa'. Those last words melted me from inside. I missed them.

Suddenly my feelings changed. I realised yes that she was right. It is just a matter of one year and that's it. After that nobody is going to stop me from doing all these things. I should have not shouted on her like this. She is doing this not for herself but for my own good.

I felt it was my mistake still I didn't apologise to her.

My pillow has seen my most honest tears. I have never been able to control my tongue. At first I shout at her but after sometimes I grasp, what I have said and comprehend, then I realise that I had made a mistake again. I really feel humiliated in apologising in front of her.

So like every person with a sensible mind, I decided to do the next logical thing, I decided to try following them from next morning.

The following day after school I checked the letter box. There were three letters that day. I checked them. One of them was a telephone bill, and then a wedding invitation which my far-flung relatives from Amritsar have sent it for their daughter's marriage and the third letter was from the ministry of Government. It was from the Prime Ministers Health Relief Fund.

My Father had written a letter to the Government of India for seeking financial help. We were still short of funds. Bhavya's operation was at risk. Only three months were left for his operation in Delhi.

I didn't dare to open that letter. I opened the other two but this one I quietly and safely kept it on my father's desk. The whole day it was revolving at the back of my mind that whether the government has agreed to sanction us the amount or not?

After dinner my father called me in his room. He asked me to read the letter for him and subsequently explain it.

For me it was the only thing I wanted to know. I wanted to know what was written in that letter.

I first had an eye reading.

Respected Sir

This letter is in correspondence with your letter dated 31/01/2014 asking for financial aid. With regret I want to state that the Government of India would be unable to provide you with the required amount. If the operation was conducted by a Government Hospital we would not have hesitated in extending you our help but according to the law we have no provision to help you when it comes to private matters.

The ministry wishes good health to your child and family.

Thank you.

I could not speak a word after I read it. It became difficult for me to explain him what was written. But I could see no other option in front of my eyes.

"Papa they are telling ki wo financial help nahi de payenge. Aur likha h ki isliye kyoki private hospital se operation kr wa rhe h agr government hota to kr dete."

In a soft voice he said okay hiding his emotions. I tried to comfort him.

We even tried to seek help from several NGO's and other organisations but our hands didn't work out anywhere.

We started losing hope. Every day was a bad page for our life. Our clock of happiness had stop.

Someone had rightly said that "In every bad situation something positive is hidden in it. Even a dead clock shows the right time two times in the day. Even if it is for a point of time but it is still there.

Our positive thing was Bhavya. Though he did not give us the solution on what has to be done but he was our light. Seeing him smile made us all forget our problems for a click of time.

The gloomy days went on. I never showed my friends what I was going through at home. But few asked about the reason behind my face.

Many of our family members offered us financial help but we faked smiles. When all the doors seemed closed my father decided to sell off Gold and Jewellery. The things even did not cover the amount so at last we sold out our car also. For medical help we took a loan of Rs. 5lac from the Bank.

Finally the total amount was gathered. It released some tension out of our mind. We didn't bother to think what could be the consequences in the future. There was no time to think whether we will be able to pay off the loan or not? The main concern as in now was his operation and we all were ready to give everything for the little boy.

A day was left when Bhavya was about to leave for his operation in Delhi. He was going for 3 months and that fact was hard to digest. I didn't know how I would be able to live without him in these 90 days. Time would pass anyway I thought.

His parents were busy downstairs with the last minute packing and so he was with me in my room.

Krishh went to bed early that night. Every day early in the morning he had his cricket sessions in the club. He wanted to be a cricketer and so he would not miss practice at any cost.

Since he was asleep Bhavya and I talked softly. Bhavya was big enough to understand things. He would make up his own questions and didn't settle for it until anyone answered it. I loved his curiosity for knowing everything. He hadn't left a question, whether it is about a flying mosquito, the rains, a mobile phone and the stars and moon in the sky.

"Bhavi mujhe teri yaad ayegi. Tu mat jaa na please." I said.

"Mujhe nahi jaana. Mujhe Doctor se darr lagtae" he replied in a soft cute voice. He did not seem to be speaking of the present but of the past. I struck by the change in tense.

"Doctor kuch nhi krte wo to ache hote h"

"Nahi hote. Wo injection. . ." his voice tailed off. His face fell down and he looked terrified and shocked.

"Ab nahi lgayenge. Main unko phone krke bol dunga ki mere Bhavya ko koi sui nahi lgayega. Theeke?"

He put his head up and smiled at me.

I took out a chocolate from my drawer and gave him. It was the first time in these years when he had rejected for a chocolate. I could make out how scared he was. I felt bad for him.

To cheer him up and to remove his fear, I played his favourite game. He would be keen to sit on my back and make me crawl in the whole house. He would act as he is the king and I am his horse. He had learned several dialogues through the TV serials and would repeat it while playing. It would not suffice him until and unless I covered the whole house.

He was completely engrossed in the game and eventually had forgotten that he would be leaving tomorrow. It took me an hour to cover each and every room that day. He cheered and laughed. Happiness really was seeing him laugh. At last he accepted my chocolate.

11/06/2014 - It was a Monday and due to the high temperatures the government had declared a holiday in the all the schools.

Before leaving from home my grandma gave them spoonful of curd and sugar. Bhavya finished the left over in one sip.

She started crying. I didn't understand the point in crying. Like they are going for a good cause and why make things monotonous from the beginning, bid farewell happily.

We arrived at the platform half-n-hour early before the train's departure time.

Before the train's departure time Mahima started crying. Seeing this, chachi also shed tears. The atmosphere became sombre. I tried to calm her.

I saw the railway clock struck 4 and then the signal turned green. It was time for the train to depart. I heard the horn of the train. I kissed and hugged Bhavya tightly. We got down from the train.

I saw him smiling at me through the window. My eyes couldn't move. It was stuck on the window. Perhaps it is not the last time I have seen the curve of his face. I prayed devotedly from inside. Two minutes after the green signal the train began its journey. I waved good bye to him. He waved back and gave the best smile ever.

I went directly towards our workplace from the railway station while Krishh and Mahima took an auto for home. Since uncle was not there I had to accompany my dad to the shop.

I have already been to the shop a number of times earlier. Papa would generally call me in the peak season when the work load was high. And now since he was all alone I had to come and help him.

My duty was to come to the shop after school till night.

That night I missed him. It was the beginning of many of those days where I would be sleeping without seeing him.

For the child he was, I once felt the sympathy which endeared Bhavya to a place in my heart and then there was no looking back.

Watching him grow has been amazing in a way where I could see my childhood in him. It's spectacular to see the young and tender emotions that flow on his face when he gets to new things. To see the joy in his eyes and hear his pure giggle when something entertains him. That desire to wonder and discover new things, that ability to love so unselfishly and without fear.

By watching him grow, I've grown. The most important thing I've realized is that the spark for life that exists in a child never dies. When you grow up, you know the pain, and loss and sufferings. You know what it feels like to be betrayed, to have your hopes crushed, to be rejected. You know what it's like to have work and obligations get in the way of you chasing your dreams. You will know all these things, which children like my brother Bhavya, is lucky enough to not know yet.

I've seen my little brother see his first sunset, take his first steps, watching his first cartoon, and right there beside him, I appreciate what it is he is experiencing for the first time as if it my own first time. I laugh with him unapologetically about something as simple as the dog chasing his tail.

I told him how and from where the sun came from and where it went, how birds build their nest and from where the rains came. He didn't understand but kept listening helplessly.

Sometimes I feel bad for Bhavya and his parents. Every month the little kid has to bear the needle and cry out in pain. He was scared of every person he met. He was afraid of injections.

I love to hug him. I thank him every time and tell him he's the best gift our family could ever be given. Though he didn't understood why I said that. I had a fear of losing him so I played with my gift as I would lose it the next day.

I remembered how I screamed around the house like him. My mind with him inadvertently reverted to the time when I used to cheat my mom into thinking I had my milk and when she came to know that I haven't I made her ran in the whole house with a glass of milk in her hand. That's how I felt when I saw him play and cry. An uneasy feeling that is a mix floating like a cloud in the mind and all those bittersweet memories bring a smile on my face.

There is no kid who has escaped this in a middle class family. Bhavya was made to wear my hand-downs. They had been carefully preserved for years waiting for my children to grow up to fit into them. My mom had preserved them, for she wanted to try those on my kids but before that Bhavya had found them in her room during Deepawali cleanings. Sometimes they were stylish, at all other times they are disgustingly unfashionable.

• • •

All these days I have hardly checked my facebook account. After a long time all I got was a few notifications and only a message. 'Forever alone'

Surprisingly it was a message from a new friend on facebook. I know her only via facebook and not in real.

The most amazing thing about her profile was that all her photos had more than 500likes. I don't know why people cared to like her photos; she is just an average looking girl.

I opened her message tab. She texted me on 19th May 'Hey :D' and then after that on 8th June again 'Hey? -.-'

I replied her 'Hey :D'

Kiarra replied immediately '12th right?'

Ujjawal: 'Yep. You took admission here? I mean SSSVV'

Kiarra: 'Yaa how do you know?'

Ujjawal: 'I just checked your profile. 'You added a life time event – started school from SSSVV'. Welcome anyway :D

So do you like in here?'

Kiarra: It is good. *_* but I don't want to come ☹'

Ujjawal: 'So why have you come? Your previous school wasn't good enough?'

Kiarra: 'Shut up it's the best school :b. Parents and subject. I have taken humanities here.'

Ujjawal: 'Haha okay. Btw how do you know me? :o'

Kiarra: I don't know you. I know your name, I searched it and you were already added'.

Ujjawal: 'weirdo -__-'

Kiarra: 'I like your hair dude.'

Ujjawal: 'Hi-fi same :'D'

    We haven't met?

Kiarra: You must have seen me I have been coming to school for one month now. You wouldn't have noticed me, did you? :b'

Ujjawal: Oh no I haven't! Never mind. I'll search for you on Monday. B|

Kiarra: Okay-Okay let's see.

Ujjawal: Bye! Nice talking to you ☺

Kiarra: same here.

On Monday I looked for her in the whole school. I searched for the one, who is small and thin, short hair, wears spectacles, not a very dark complexion, the one with a dimple on the right cheek when she smiles. The whole school time I had Kiarra in my mind. I don't know why I was so desperate to see her.

Unfortunately I had not seen her.

I went home and relaxed on the bed. In my mind I tried to cross check her profile picture with every girl I had seen in the school. But I couldn't figure out. May be I had not seen her or even if I how I missed her. Thinking all this I don't know when I slept.

In the evening after accounts class I checked my facebook. There was her message.

Kiarra: so did you notice me?

Ujjawal: No. I looked for you the whole day but no -.-

Kiarra: Liar. We even had eye contacts twice.

Ujjawal: -_- Oh let me think. Our eyes met near the pillar at the entrance right?

Kiarra: yes!

Ujjawal: Seriously. I can't believe this, you look so different. I mean you look fabulous in pictures and you in reality LOL :'D

Kiarra: Katti -.-

Ujjawal: :'D LOL. Sorry.

We soon exchanged our phone numbers. So I didn't have to wait for her to come online. This limited our everyday chats on facebook. Whenever I or she wished to talk we would text each other on direct messages. Slowly I started enjoying talking with her. She was very ready to talk to me and answer my any question I asked her, we would discuss about all the things in the world. My and her opinions never matched on anything and so almost all the time we ended up fighting.

She was cute. She would always appreciate me in small-small things. I enjoyed it when it came to the flirting part.

We never talked in the school. She was too shy to approach and I also didn't mind that.

Chapter 9

Teenybopper

It was late in the night when I got home tired from work. I realized how much difficult it was for my dad to earn a penny for us. He had to give in day and night to make a living.

The worst part of the thing in those days was that I had to manage both my studies and mark presence at the shop.

It became really tough for me to balance things.

That day Papa gave the news that Doctors are through with the proceedings. They have admitted Yash today in the evening for extracting his DNA.

While I was getting myself comfortable to get under the blanket, I had a text message from Kiarra. She asked me to check my facebook account when I was free.

I gathered all my strength and headed to my parent's room to access my computer.

"What is the need to access your computer right now?" Mom queried when I turned on the computer.

"Mom I have to check some important e-mails from school" I replied.

I first opened my mail account just to make her feel that I really had some e-mails to check. After five minutes in time I switched over to facebook. I opened her message.

'All the party freaks. Get up and put on your clothes and dancing shoes because it's freaking time to rock the floor at the New Red Lounge. The opening ceremony presents India's most rated artist DJ Sunny. We welcome you with complimentary Vodka shots, veg and non-veg starters and unlimited beer and cocktails for limited hours.

22nd June Doors open at 4PM.

For bookings contact. . .. . .' Male or female stag – 1000 and Couple- 1200.

Days were so boring and she had come up with a party at the right time.

I checked my wallet. I was short of 700 bucks. I did not felt like asking for money from my father. He had already told us to save funds. I respect him.

I replied her 'Okay! That is too pricey for me and I won't be able to come sorry'. ☺

I had not told her about my situation. I wish I could make her understand how things were with me at home.

Kiarra: Please come!

Me: I'll see.

Kiarra: Okay let me know. If you want to come I'll save some for you.

Me: For free? 'That was out of curiosity'

Kiarra: Yes dude for FREE B|. It's my best friend's party.

And when she said this I instantly made up my mood for the party.

Me: Hahaha okay. Still I will let you know. Anyway good night I am too sleepy.

Kiarra: Yep! Goodnight.

Ujjawal: Btw will you watch today's match?

Today Brazil was going to play Mexico in the group stage. The world cup fever was on everywhere.

Kiarra: Yes yes yes.

Ujjawal: Yayaya I will too. Keep your phone near you we'll chat ;)

Kiarra: Sure ;) now go! Bye

Ujjawal: Bye :'D

I didn't talk to my parents about the party after that and went to my bedroom. I set an alarm for 3:30 in my phone for the world cup football match. Kiarra and I were diehard fans of Brazil. For years I was looking for that girl who could talk football and cricket with me.

I woke up at 4 by a call.

"Hello. Who is this?" I said in a half sleep voice.

"Arre get up. It's me Kiarra. Don't you wish to watch the game huh?"

"Oh damn! I didn't hear the alarm Thank you" She hung up.

I saw her 6 text messages; I messaged her 'Sorry'. I went to the washroom. After I came I checked my phone again for her message.

I saw a pop up notification on my mobile screen 'This message cannot be sent. You are running out of balance' my phone confirmed.

I went in to the drawing room downstairs.

I very quietly switched on the TV. I saw the score. It was all square at 0-0 at 35th minute.

Then I took my landline and called her.

"Listen I am sorry again. I am running out of balance in my phone so I can't text"

"what the. . . man? I woke up because. . .." She replied in a hasty voice.

"Because. . . What?" I heard the last line in my heart, but my ears wanted to hear it loud and clear.

"Nothing let me sleep now goodnight" she said.

"But aren't you watching the match?"

"No. It's too boring" she exclaimed.

"Okay! Tell me, why you woke up?

"Bye"

"Sleep then good night bye"

"Bye"

"Wait Wait Listen, listen, listen. Guess what I am coming to the party"

"YAAYYYY" She cheered over the phone. "So shall I bring the passes for you tomorrow."

"Yeah! Sure why not"

"Collect it then. Bye"

Afterwards I had a message from her again.

'Thank you for coming. You are so cute and awesome.'

She had been doing it the entire summer. She would find combinations for me. Sometimes cute and funny, smart and handsome, and the best were crazy and lazy. I smiled at it.

It was 5:30 in the morning. Brazil won it 2-0. Still there was one hour's time for me to get up according to my parents. I went and slept.

When I came down for my break-fast mom scolded me for watching the match. She got to know that I was awake for the match.

I had carelessly left my dish and glass on the table and forgot to put it back in the kitchen. She also saw some chips on the floor.

I went to school half dead. I was too sleepy. I wanted to sleep more. Yesterdays match gave me nothing.

I looked for her in the school because I wanted to collect the passes for the party. But gosh she was absent. I knew she would have got late and missed her bus. If it is like that then it would be her 6th time.

I went home and messaged her 'You missed your bus again haina?'

She replied 'Bade log! Sab Ptae apko toh. You already know that the bus arrives too early :'(. Anyway I'll come tomorrow then take it. ;)'

'Oh madam I'll not come to you. You come and give it to me.'

'This is not fair. I'll not come.'

Let's see who comes to choose.

The following day in the school I saw her. I remained firm with my words. We both had multiple eye contacts. Our eyes were fighting with each other.

Nobody took a step forward. At the end while going home I saw her looking at me through the bus window. We smiled at each other. She and I communicated million words through our face expressions. It was fun to irritate her.

Kiarra: 'You go and Die.'

Me: 'I already told you I won't come. You have to come and give me.'

Kiarra: 'I also said that. Okay listen if you don't come tomorrow to me I won't give you the pass in any case. Final'

Me: 'lalalala lets see.'

Kiarra: 'If you seriously want it come and take it in the short break in front of my class XI-F.'

Ujjawal: 'If you want me to come to the party come and give me those passes in front of my class XII-D in the short break.'

Kiarra: 'This is cheating ;b'

Ujjawal: Hahaha. Anyway I want to change my current profile picture. It's too old. I want to get clicked with you and use that photo for my profile picture. ;) Is that okay with you?'

I wanted a photo with her only because I wanted more likes on my facebook picture. Till now I was struggling to touch 70.

Kiarra: 'Good joke. Tell me one more I can't stop laughing.'

Ujjawal: Die 5ft. Kiarra, I am not kidding you.'

Kiarra: 'Oh 5ft 7inches are you serious you want a profile picture with me? And that means you'll collect the pass tomorrow.'

Ujjawal: 'Yes I am serious but not about the pass thing. Bye and Thank you once again.'

Kiarra: 'Bye and please tomorrow take it or else. . . you can understand.'

The following day in the short break I came out of my class. I saw her with her classmates in front of class XI F.

I knew she won't come so I started my marching towards her class. She understood that I was coming to her to take the passes. As soon as she saw me turn towards the corridor which leads to her classroom she detached from her group. I saw her coming towards me.

Till now I was really going to her to collect the pass but those lines struck my mind. As we were just few steps away from each other I took my eyes from her. I took some quick steps forward and instead of walking straight I turned left towards the dining hall.

I didn't look back after that and took the stairs. I wanted to see her expression. What she had thought and what I did. She must have stood completely blank.

After crossing the dining hall I quickly ran towards my class. I wanted to see her impulse on what I have just done.

Raj didn't understand anything what I just did. I said him to keep quiet and that I'll explain him everything later.

I saw her in a black mood. She just wanted a chance to beat me up for doing this. I put my right hand on my ear and said sorry.

I told Raj what happened in the economics lecture. Ma'am had seen us talking and thus scolded us. The next time she saw us talking again and she removed us out of the class. We enjoyed our punishment as it gave us a good chance to finish the topic and talk more. As a junior student I was always scared of these punishments but now things had changed.

Our Business Studies lecturer left the class late. But finally I was able to collect passes from her when the buses were about to leave. I gave some chocolates to her and apologised.

In My Eternity

While I was at the shop, I was thinking on how I should tell dad about the tomorrow's party and that I want to go. The biggest problem was that the party day was a Sunday and Papa would never give me a leave on Sunday because it was the core day of the business.

Also earlier in the day when I arrived he had a diatribe with one of his supplier for not completing the order on time so I waited for his mood swing. In the day I didn't get the right time to ask him.

In the evening I called mom and asked her to cook his favourite dish so that I can have a word with him before I go to sleep.

I didn't talk to him at the dining table because I knew if I talk in front of my mom she is definitely going to reject my request. I waited again.

Finally I saw him calmed and suffice after taking his food.

When mom was busy clearing the kitchen I asked him "Papa I have to go to the party tomorrow. It's my best friend's birthday so please. . .?"

He cut me in between and said "Hahaha beta kal to Sunday h." The line was self explanatory.

"Papa please! I'll go only for an hour. I promise" I requested.

"At what time is your party?" he questioned me.

"In the evening."

"If it could have been in the afternoon I would have not said you anything but it is in the evening when the work load is high and I need you. Sorry"

"Dad please, he is my best friend."

I was fortunate that he didn't ask me his name. He said nothing and concentrated on his favourite stock market program.

"Dad please shall I go?" I disturbed him after 5 minutes of silence.

"I said no before and I am saying it again." I said nothing and left the hall.

I was reading my novel when mom came inside my room. She closed the door behind sensitively.

While setting the bed for the night she asked me "Konse friend ki party hai?" "hai ek" I answered back.

"Don't worry, go I'll talk to your dad" she confirmed.

"What?" I closed the book in my hand in a flash and turned my chair towards her.

"Mom how can you say that. Don't you remember those rules?" I taunted pointing my finger towards them.

"Yes I know but since it's your best friend's party I am allowing you to go and it's the last time."

I felt a little indecision that why I am lying to her while she is taking my side. A girl has invited me and it was no best friend's party. It was a date.

"And who will go to the shop tomorrow?" I asked frivolously.

"I'll send Krishh. I had a word with him just now."

"Wow awesome. That is really awesome. Thank you so much."

I read the novel till 2:30 and then watched the world cup match.

When I got up I saw Mom was not home. She had locked the main door from outside and I was left with nothing. I didn't care to phone her and ask where she had gone and at what time she'll be back? All I wanted was to sleep again.

I got up when I heard her shouting at me.

"Uth jaa nalayak kitna soyega" It was the Indian way of asking your child to leave the bed. I looked for my phone. After years of finding it I asked her about my phone.

"Haa jeb main h meri aake le le. Aur subah subah bhagwaan k darshan krne chahiye ki phone ke"

"Subah to kab ki ho gyi h abhi dufer h. Btao yr mera phone kaha h?"

"It's in my room. Don't you dare touch it? First go and take your bath. I am preparing your lunch".

After lunch I struggled hard in choosing my party clothes.

I had taken a red shirt, black trousers and loafers as my evening dress.

I saw her coming up the escalator after 15 minutes of my arrival, she looked beautiful. She was dressed to kill. I don't remember what she was wearing as I was already undressing her.

We took the entry and I jumped on the starters first. She met with her friends meanwhile. Thereupon she introduced me to all of them. A bit later, her friends dragged me to the dance floor. I wanted to give everything tonight and return myself with a pack. Though I was quite late for my first date but I craved to achieve great heights from there.

At first, there were just bits of information about all of them so it took us some time to get used to ourselves.

An hour more into the party when we all had drained ourselves into shots of beer and vodka, we all danced crazy. All were pumped up, it was like go bananas. That is what we were put in for, on the dance floor. Kiarra and I clicked a number of photos with her iPhone. It is when I understood why she was hot in all her Facebook photographs. iPhone + Girls = Hot pictures.

Everybody got separated within a span of time giving some or the other reason and I was left with the one who had been hitting on me since the beginning. When I started to get a bit uncomfortable with her just then Kiarra returned and took her, she asked me not to follow her. I made myself comfortable on the sofa after that.

In breadth of time when nobody came back, I took out my phone out to ask them to join me. I saw her message was already there. 'Won't be able to make up, I will tell you everything in school.'

I called her to know what happened all of a sudden. Her phone was switched off. I then returned home. I had a whale of time but then what's an event without a drama. Late night, I dropped her messages on facebook.

Chapter 10

She or 12ᵗʰ Boards?!

The subsequent day in the school I met her and Kavya during the recess. She told me why they had to leave the party so urgently.

"So why you people lied?"

"Then they won't have allowed us." she said.

"What about your phone, why didn't you reply?"

"The phone is with dad and you know what he had slapped me also."

"Oh! Anyway I also deluded my parents that it is my best friend's party." She gave a Hi-fi.

"Listen we won't be able to talk now until my phone is back so will you meet me in the recess every day? We'll talk please." She demanded.

I liked her appeal. It was like she was every day dragging me towards her. It was how comfortable I was with her. The way I was with the way she was, a perfect tie.

I didn't promise her that I will but I confirmed to her that I'll try.

Alternately, I and Kiarra met in the recess. My friends now started believing that there was something between me and her. Her classmates would also doubt about us.

It was frustrating for me. People took me close to her and more I missed our day night chatting. In a day I would hear more than 100 beeps on my phone. For her my message voucher changed from Rs.50 to Rs.128 per month.

After a long break of 15 days her dad had given her phone back. As she got the phone she forwarded three of our photos to me on facebook.

Me: 'Chhii.'

Kiarra: 'It is nice, shut up. Btw which one will you upload?'

Me: 'By looking at them I don't wish to upload any one.'

Kiarra: 'You have to. Please' she begged.

Me: 'They are not good.'

Kiarra: 'I'll edit it and give. You wait.'

She edited all the three pictures and forwarded them to me. I was still confused in selecting which one to upload. I did 'Akad bakad Bambe bo' like I used to do for selecting things in my childhood.

As always my index finger would end on the thing which I unloved the most. This time too 'Akad Bakad Bambey bo' ended on the worst picture and like always I didn't choose what my index finger pointed at, it was always my own choice.

I added the photo.

Me: 'Done. Happy?'

Kiarra: 'Yes.'

She was the first to like and comment on it. She commented 'Awesome you look :*'

When I reached home I checked the likes, comments and messages. Within 8 hours I had 120 likes. I had more than 100 likes. The job was done.

I had a message that day from Vedant, her classmate.

'Kya Ujjwal bhai, kya scene h tera or Kiarra ka? Dp wagera daal rhe ho'.

Then after 10 mins there was another message 'Dur rehna usse, dhang se Bol raha hun haina, Samjh le. Mujhe tujhse koi problem nahi hai bas usse dur rehna or jaise hi msg padhe, pic delete ho jaani chahiye.'

I don't know what he wanted? I thought may be Kiarra and he were in a relationship before that is why he was jealous or maybe he likes her and wants a relationship with her now. But damn how can he like her? Oh what am I saying? She would have told me if she is aware of it. Why I am so concerned? Shit I'll talk to her in the school tomorrow.

The enduring thoughts scrolled my mind.

Next day in the school as I entered the class everyone teased me by her name and then there were different comments too. Kiarra and I became a hot topic in the school.

'Bawahaha DP'

'Recess main bhi kha khelta h aaj kl'

'Dikha di isne dosti sala bhaag hi gya na ladki k peeche' and this one was my favourite 'Ab to Ujjawal apn ko bhool hi jayega.'

Though these lines were irritating but when it knocked into my ears, every time her smiling face flashed my mind.

I tried to make my friends understand that she was my no girlfriend nevertheless a BESTFRIEND.

Like always we met in the recess, I asked her about this Vedant.

She told she was too frustrated with him. He had already proposed her two times before and he had a crush on her even before she joined the school.

Kiarra didn't like him. She had already fallen for someone else and when I cared to ask who the lucky boy is she said nothing.

Vedant was not attending the school from the past one week. If he had not been out of station I would have open and shut the case then and there itself. I was being protective.

When I reached home I again had a message from him 'Bhai I told you to delete the picture' I read the message and marked it as unread.

Now it was going beyond a limit.

Thinking a lot on the matter I replied him. 'You meet me in the school whenever you are coming to Indore.'

I stayed up with my friends that night. Harsh was also there.

I started accepting him again as my brother since the day Summer and I found something between us.

"Kiarra has a serious crush on you." He said encouragingly. I was really shocked when I heard that. It made me wobble.

"This cannot happen dude her. . . Do you have any proof?" I asked him.

He took out his phone and showed a screenshot.

Damn if she likes me she should have told me why she is bragging it around other people? I was being childish that honesty and friendships were important these days but the new trend was all about being secretive and shady.

If I had fallen for her I would have said her straight. She had fallen for me and shit 'Am I the one?'

It was never expected and I was not ready for a relationship. The rule no. 1 was the only thing I decided to follow in my class 12th and till now I didn't followed any of them.

On Monday Kavya was absent. She had hurt her leg in an accident.

I felt a bit uncomfortable when she asked me to take a walk with her in the school avenue.

"Ujjawal I am itching to tell you this since so long" I understood what she wanted to say. My beats raised.

"I am in love with you." She admitted after a long pause and in between I was thinking about the screenshot that Harsh showed me some nights before.

She felt my Goosebumps when my hand accidently touched her. She would have understood there itself that how much those words weigh for me.

She fell in love.

I didn't.

There was altogether a different feeling when I read that line that 'I have a crush on Ujjawal' and then in her tone 'I am in love with you'.

The situation presented itself with a dilemma, propounded; I didn't want to unlike her nor want to love her. I wanted everything to be neutral.

I don't want to lose her because I loved her as a friend? No a Best Friend actually.

I also recalled that my priorities had changed suddenly within a short time. I was already fed up with the rumours which were spreading in the school regarding us and then there was Vedant.

I was sure I was going to spoil my twelfth result. I had to stop all these somehow. It all seemed like I was addicted to wasting time. Even if it is true that she is in love with me I make sure that I won't take a step forward. It's my twelfth and I won't risk it for these silly things.

I didn't know much about love but one thing I definitely know is that it had spoiled many 12th class results.

It is time I need to get up again. If I don't go after what I want I'll never have it. If I don't look for the answers now I'll never going to achieve it. If I don't step forward I'll always be in the same place.

I was scared of love that it will ruin my twelfth. There was that undying fear of failure.

But above all it was happy to see that someone really cares for me. I wished I could her hug that time.

We don't exchanged words until we turned back. "And when did it happen?" I replied after some thought.

She gave a blank look. "I don't know but maybe after the party I started admiring you a lot"

I didn't knew that she would store our everyday chats in her heart, that the glass of beer would developed her liking for me, that the DJ would let her fall in love with me, that those little-little moments would matter somewhere and then she would never look back.

Heavy rains started down. It spoiled the whole mood. We ran towards the shelter. She went to her classroom then and I to mine.

When I got home I messaged her and explained her everything that why 'NO'.

I promised myself to be her good friend and that I'll propose to her after my 12th boards.

Chapter 11

Moments under the Sun

He hung up the phone; I saw a real smile on my father's face after a long time. Finally the important and the major part of the operation were concluded.

Bhavya's operation was a great triumph. It was an unspoken success for us.

How satisfied my uncle and aunt's would be there I thought. The doctors were finished but we were not. Half the work was done. The actual task had started now.

The doctors prescribed that we need to take his utmost care. It's like a new life which is given to him. It's like his second birth. He has to be as safe as a child is safe in her mother's womb. A small infection like cold could make things same as before.

Although things were still really hard to deal with that moment but we had hope out of hope that we'll see Bhavya in a better position when he comes back from Delhi.

Uncle had taken a flat on rent. Different conditions were made ready for Bhavya. The room was cleaned 3 times thoroughly before his arrival. Only a double bed was kept with nothing in the room. Only his mother could visit him inside and that too with the mouth covered. The doctor gave cumbersome restrictions on eating various foodstuffs. Only normal home-made food was allowed on his tongue. No mobile phones or any electronics were to surround him. These things were to be adhered to for one complete month.

After few days he was discharged from the hospitals when his body started producing healthy blood. Grandma remained in Delhi, for control over household work.

It was still time to see happy faces back again.

Mahima and my second uncle visited them in Delhi after he was brought home (flat in Delhi). Unfortunately I could not go because something great and splendid thing was on my way. I was forced to stay here.

The day had come. I had waited for this moment hard under the sun. It came pretty late though.

I got up fifteen minutes early from the bed. I went out on the terrace for the fresh air. Everything was calm and peaceful beginning to take life. Today was a going to be a memorable day at school. After a long time I had seen the sun rising.

All I wanted was to look good today. I had dressed quite nicely that day with my collar button on and tie perfectly shaped. I got ironed my uniform twice from mummy so that I am not left with a crush on it. I polished my shoes as I rarely do. I put my blazer on. I had dressed like I was going to walk on the Red Carpet today. But the upcoming event was not going to be less for me. I sat in front of the mirror combing my hair. Every time when I got ready for school I have spent 10 minutes of the day in front of the mirror with my hair. And every time my mom asked me the same question "You go to school to study or to do fashion? Huh."

The school auditorium was luminous today. It was full of light. Everything was set for the Investiture ceremony. We were also set. Today all the council members were to be handed over their batches. It was my first time on stage in front of crowd of over 1000 people.

It was sort of an odd thing for me. I have never experienced how it's like to be on the stage throughout my school life.

I feared that I don't commit a mistake with the actions while marching towards the podium and then excited at the same time that I would be handed over the badge in front of the whole school and specially she.

I had frequent eye contacts with her during the whole assembly. Whenever I looked at her my cheek flushed and heart raced faster. I was caught smiling at her by my Accounts sir but he didn't mind it.

The anchors started with the words of wisdom after the assembly. They requested the Honourable Director Sir, Principal ma'am and the Vice Principal ma'am for their presence on the dais.

The drummer played the marching beats. It was the Head Boy's chance first.

Aryan began marching with his chest broad towards the centre. He looked tall that day. He had the best biceps in school at that time. We both used to go to the gym after our coaching's. I didn't work on my biceps but was keen on my abs and I had already impressed the school girls by uploading a picture of them on facebook earlier that summer. The Director Sir pinned him the batch on left side of his blazer. They shook hands and then Aryan step backward and marched beside the Principal.

After him the Head Girl Jiya marched towards the centre.

She too was no less. She had been to Nationals and Indian Camp for basketball thrice. I was encouraged by her play. She indirectly inspired me to play basketball.

The school's Deputy Head Boy, Deputy Head Girl, Sports Captain, Sports vice Captain were given the badges.

It was now turn of the House Captains. This time the captains were not selected by the house guides and teachers but by the students. There was pen and paper voting where in suitable candidates of their house represented them in the house elections. It was all like the Lok Sabha Elections where in we had to deliver the speech as candidate does and attract the audience. And the best part was to go and join hands in front of them and promise them things. I had worked hard for the later part.

The other Captains were done. It was our turn now.

My heart beat raised as the drummer lifted the stick to beat the drum. The first drum sent a shiver down my spine. The whole school had their eyes focused on us.

I took my left leg forward and we both marched towards the centre. I missed what the anchors said about me. It gave a happy feeling when I heard my first set of clap from the audience.

I stood in front of her, my back towards the audience. She smiled elegantly at me. Principal ma'am pinned the batch on my blazer and then placed the Pragati House Captain Sash around my neck.

It was light but seemed heavy. I shook hands with her, turned back and marched. I did it well.

We the captains lined up adjacent to each other on the stage. Boys were on one side and Girls on another. We waited until the people under our thumb i.e. the house vice captains, house sports captain and others of our House were given their batches.

After they had completed the cherry picked Head Girl went on the dais for the oath taking ceremony. She commanded us to lift our right hand and repeat after her.

That was an exotic moment. I had Goosebumps when I repeated those lines. I was not familiar with these lines before and yet they had hit me hard down in the centre. Those lines meant something to me perhaps because I was chosen by my house students and friends. Now I had a liability a big liability to prove them that yes they were right in selecting me, they had believed in me and I would pay off well to them by taking my house on the top position in the end.

For the first time my shoulders were too much heavy with responsibility. I had felt it the moment I got my badge.

I would work harder, fight for glory and write my own story in the end. Absolutely nothing can stop me.

The school band played the National Anthem to mark the end of ceremony.

Mahima and I arrived at the same time. I came from school and she arrived from Delhi.

As per the news from the Capital they were to get back home within two weeks.

The thing brought intense excitement in me. I was over thrilled to welcome him back home after almost two months. I had missed each and everything without him whether it is from watching cartoons or eating a chocolate with him.

Mahima showed his photos. She clicked them from a distance. He looked cute. It was nice to see him again after so many days.

Chapter 12

Trauma

I have Cherophobia. I am afraid of being too happy because I am every time nervous that very soon dark clouds are going to eliminate my delight. There had been times in my life when darkness has leapt over it. There had been moments when I enjoyed the happiness and someone swept it away. As I thought of Euphoria, things became more complex for me.

It was another illogical fear living in me.

It happened again. This time it was the most unpleasant thing to happen to me on this earth. Not only me but to all my family members.

It was in the afternoon taking lunch when I saw papa enter through the main door. He was looking dull.

At first I didn't see anything. When I asked why he came so early from work, he didn't respond. I looked at him and he was weeping. I stood up and left my food.

"Mummy Mummy Mummy. . ." I called her. She was in the kitchen. She left everything in her hand and came to the drawing room.

She sat near him. "suno kya hua, ro kyo rhe ho. Ujjawal jaldi jaa paani lekr aa papa k liye"

I went quickly and fetched a glass of water for him. I saw him still crying. He drank it peacefully and said "Bhavya. . .Infection" he said half heartedly.

"Shit" I punched the sofa.

"Oh God"

It felt like my heart was no more. It was something bolt from the blue.

Fortunately Mahima slept because she was tired after her journey and she didn't heard anything what he said.

He calmed down after five minutes. "Diarrhoea hua hai" he exploded.

It was only ten days after his operation and he got infection.

In the evening he reported the whole matter to the rest of the family members in depth. Bhavya was again admitted in the hospital that afternoon.

As much as I can comprehend Bhavya's intestines were weak.

In the last ten operations it was the first case where in diarrhoea was recorded. The infection was fatal and the chances of survival were less.

Papa didn't go to the shop after that. He was all the day in his room making calls every hour at Delhi. He was talking with Doctors if there is a way out or if something can happen? He was ready to give each and everything.

Two days into to the hospital and he was not able to recover. The situations got worsen. With ongoing Diarrhoea his body stopped making blood. Alas the operation failed. Now we only prayed that his life is saved nothing more than that.

My body shivered when Bhavya's thought raced my mind. It seemed like I had lost all my strength. He was the one whom I loved more than any of my family people.

I cried when nobody was there, I laughed with his memories all alone, for me these days were really insufferable. There was so much on my mind. I could feel how much he would have missed me in these days. My heart every time seemed heavy. I was not ready to accept jokes or any of those sorts when I was with my friends.

It was like how I can laugh when my whole family is crying there. I was experiencing life at a rate of several Why's. I started avoiding play, music, friends and everything. My source of happiness became my problems.

My last word with him was only a Good bye at the railway station and after that we had didn't exchange a single word. My ears waited eagerly to hear his voice. I had continuous three days off at school so I requested dad that I want to go and meet Bhavya. He agreed he knew my everyday face could make out how depressed and stressed I was.

A day before my train I planned to meet Kiarra.

. . .

I along with the other council members stood adjacent to each other near the place where the flag was going to be hoisted.

It was a tradition in the school that whosoever the 12th topper is for the previous session that student would be invited as a chief guest on the Independence Day to hoist the flag.

In My Eternity

She came in the traditional Indian dress. She had scored 97.2% in her 12th with Commerce + Maths stream.

The young lady with purpose moved towards the Flag. The school band played the beats to begin the National Anthem.

I saw her unfurling the flag through her hands. My heartfelt a feeling of hard work and determination and I promised myself that I'll be in that position in the next year.

As the cultural program ended Kiarra, Kavya, Raj and I covertly departed from the premises. Yesterday because of the rains we had to cancel the plan in the last minute.

I told them the whole story and the reason of me going to Delhi that day. They were sad to hear about Bhavya.

We discussed more on the topic while having our coffee and some snacks.

While Raj and Kavya went in the parking lot for taking their vehicles, I and Kiarra stood outside the cafe waiting for them.

"I already told you there is something. Why did you didn't tell me about Bhavya? It's been so many days." She scolded me.

"I did not wanted to make you feel concerned for me."

"But indirectly you had by not sharing." We didn't speak until they both came.

"Don't worry Ujjawal. Everything would be fine. Bhavya would get back home in a good condition". She did this every time. She never left a sentence in our conversation that would make me feel better than before. I made a sign of conformity and smiled.

I went home and did the packing. Mom dropped me at the railway station on time.

As I walked towards the compartment I thought of Bhavya who few months ago walked with me hand in hand at the station. The circumstances were different now.

I took my window seat and I purchased a book from the bookstall for my overnight journey. The train started with its journey and I with the novel in my hand.

As the train picked up speed the book picked up my interest. I was fond of Love stories.

While reading the book I kept on chatting with Kiarra. I was so buried in the book and then her messages that I never came to know when the dusk passed and the stars covered the sky. It was until when one uncle who was sitting near me requested me to take my dinner as it was almost time to pack up things and sleep.

I took my dinner and then the lights were switched off. I had no chance left to read the remaining half part of the novel under no light.

I was left with nothing to do with. I plugged my earphones and eagerly waited for tomorrow to come fast. I slept thinking about what could be later part of the book.

I got up and got to know that the train just crossed Faridabad and was into the outskirts of the capital. An hour more and I'll get to see him after a long wait.

The train reached the Nizamuddin Railway station. I went out and quickly hired a paid taxi to Karol Bagh. I directed the taxi driver for the exact place as uncle directed me on the phone.

Finally I saw him standing just outside the big edifice. The building touched the high sky. BL KAPOOR HOSPITAL it read on the top with block letters.

As I got down I hugged him. For so many days he was looking for something like this. He wanted patience, he wanted someone from the home to come and give him comfort like this. He was my best friend in the house and it was my responsibility to stand with my friend and face the problem together.

"Chalo pehle hospital" I said.

"Abhi kaha se. Milne ka time 10 se 2 rehta h fir sham ko 5-7"

There were still 3 hours left. With nowhere to go he took me to the flat in which they accommodated. It was at a five minute walk from the hospital.

The door was half open, I entered. I saw Yash. He was busy with himself doing nothing.

"Yash"

He looked up and gave the biggest smile. He was kind of surprised to see me here. I went towards Dadi and touched her feet.

I sat and talked with them for few minutes. I tried to know how life was like in Delhi. Yash was bored. He had nothing to do the whole day. Usually TV was his favourite time pass when he was in Indore but they there had no such things. Still he could not believe the fact that I was here. He kept on asking me questions.

I looked inside the room where Bhavya was brought in. It was as it was told.

Yet it was kept clean as Bhavya would come back again but who knows what God has in his pockets for all of us.

I got fresh and bathed quickly. Within that time Dadi prepared the breakfast. My quest grew even more as the clock kept ticking.

She served the dish with 'Aloo ka parantha'. She already knew they were my most liked.

After a peaceful breakfast we went to the hospital. The security guard checked me from top to bottom. Every time I had to go under a security check I wished to say 'Oh yes I am one of the man of Osama Bin Laden and I wish to bomb this place. I am coming over you people.'

But here I didn't play the prank thinking they would really throw me out of the property. A minute of scrutiny and the big moustache guard gave me entry through the gates. We took the elevator for the 8th floor.

I filled in the records of the visitor as I got down from the lift. Then the medical staff handed me some clothes to wear. It had an orange coat, and a cloth like monkey cap which covered whole my up except nose and eyelids. I entered room no. '808'.

He lay quietly on the bed with his eyes directed on the TV screen. His face had lost the natural touch. His whole body had joints of tubes which lead to a different bottle. His body had marks of operation. He had gone completely darkish.

I sat on the stool next to his bed for few minutes. I tried to share a word with him but he didn't responded. Maybe he didn't recognise me as I had my face covered but then doesn't he remember my voice?

In My Eternity

The nurse came in the room for recording his results. She instructed me not buzz around Doraemon and next time if she sees me in the circumference of 2 meters from the bed she is going to throw me down from the 8th floor. I don't know was that really a warning or a sarcastic comment. Never mind Bhavya smiled when she said it.

The medical staff called him Doraemon. They kept this name because for his love for cartoons.

I changed my place and sat on the fluffy sofa. I removed the thing which covered my face as it was too suffocating.

I brought his old toy before I left for Delhi. It was his favourite Doraemon piggy bank.

I shook it with my hands to draw his attention. The jingling of the coins moved his attention towards me. He cried for his money.

The time flew quickly. The hour hand was about to hit one in a couple of minutes but till now Bhavya didn't talk to me and in the whole time I made attempts to hear a word from his mouth for me.

"Why is he doing this to me? Why isn't he talking?" I exclaimed.

"He is depressed. Sitting still under a four cornered room for so many days had a minor effect on his brain. And like before he is not sharing any words with us also. He has gone completely quiet."

"Will he get out of it then?" I questioned.

"Yes but once he gets that open exposure again."

101

When I asked questions about his health and in how many days he would get back home he gave me strange answers. The answers were not connected with each other.

His facial expression talked more than his words. I was sure he was hiding something from me something more serious about his health.

I was in Delhi for that day only and once if I left the hospital there was no chance to visit him again. I made frantic efforts in front of him to talk to me. I broke the order which that nurse had given me. I sat back adjacent to his bed.

"Bhavya Bhavya ek bar baat krle please. Dekh mujhe teri itni yaad ati h. Tujhe ati h meri yaad?"

Despite continuous efforts from my side and from his parent's side he didn't spoke. Unfortunately the visiting time was up by 5 minutes and it was time for me to leave him.

I gathered all my things and kept them into my small hand bag. I bid a goodbye to chachi and then to Bhavya.

My legs felt heavy as I walked towards the door. Without doubt I didn't wish to leave the place and him under such condition.

I was ready to take care of him all throughout the day. I wanted them for once get back home and sleep pacefully.

Their eyes showed how tensed they were. Forget all what was going on. I wanted them to get back to the happy days. I wanted to be a part of healing.

I opened the door to the way out. I turned back again with a hope that this time he would listen to me. Not from his ears but from his heart.

I took wrong steps. I kneeled down in front of him. He looked towards me.

"Bhavi tu jaldi se theek ho ja aur ghar pe a jaa uske baad apan in doctors ko bht marenge. Inne teko sui lgai na apn inki khoob pitai krenge theeke."

He laughed but not with the same zeal and liveliness like before. He placed his soft tender hands on my face and that was zenith, a peak of happiness.

He smiled as I left the room.

Later in the day chachu and I took lunch in the nearby restaurant and after that we went out on the streets of the Capital. I took him out because I wanted him to feel at rest and enjoy better things in this world for a point of time.

In the evening we haunted the famous 'Gaffar Market'. I shopped some casuals for me and Krishh. Whenever I visited Delhi I hoarded a bag full of Juju beans for me and for Bhavya for the whole year. This time too I purchased them in bulk.

I completed the novel when I got home. I opened the book some days ago and after 324 pages it opened my mind on what Love is?

Even after my arrival here in Indore I everyday called in Delhi to know about his position.

It was one month on the hospital bed and Bhavya was still fighting for his life. The extra expenses were never planned. We afforded to the point we could but after that the doctor excused us for not paying the bill amount. We were extremely grateful to the hospital team for their benevolent outlook.

One day Papa took a different route for home. He stopped at an agents firm who books online tickets. He came after two minutes and then we headed back home.

At home he told that he had booked three tickets in Tatkal {urgent} for the next day and he along with my brother and one cousin uncle would go and meet Bhavya.

Everyone in the house had met or was going to meet the little kid. But my mom never forced or compelled or requested anyone that she too longed to see him. She was also a member of the house and ultimately his second mother. Burdened by the household circumstances she withholds her decision. That was one thing I understood in all those days when she talked about Bhavya to me in her free time. She would look at the old photos and videos time and again.

Papa and Krishh at last reached Delhi. According to what Krishh told me on phone after attending Bhavya at the hospital was that Bhavya became weaker and most probably the Doctors have given up things. Papa and chachu both went to the senior doctors to know if anything could save his life. He was ready to throw everything that we had.

The whole thing gave me so much frustration that I could not swallow a single bite of food down my throat.

To divert my mind I talked to her. Day by day my bonding with Kiarra grew stronger. I wanted her to be my now. But the situation that I was going through never allowed me to take a step forward. I was on the urge of getting someone and on the other hand urge of losing someone.

I was sitting in the drawing room teaching Mahima mathematics in the evening. Mom came running from upstairs.

"Ujjawal doctors ne jawab de diya h. Ek do din main Bhavya. . ." her gestures in the end conveyed his end. It made my blood run cold.

I already knew it. I had never told mom what Krishh had told me earlier in the day. I was upset.

I saw mom hiding tears from Mahima. She went in the kitchen.

I concluded her revision session after what I heard. She deliberately asked me about what mom just told about Bhavya.

"He is going to be fine soon nothing else. You don't worry" I said.

I went inside the Kitchen and asked who had told her about this?

"Massi ne bola. Tere chachu aur papa ke aankho main aasu a gye the." Obviously it had to happen. After all he is our blood.

I went to the terrace. Balls of water dipped in salt rolled down my cheeks. I shed tears under the setting dusk. For one hour I stood there crying and thinking about all the whys?

I went to the Gurudwara after that. I never believed in God and it was the first time when I walked myself to the holy place. I kneeled down and cried.

""Where are you? Don't you feel pity for us? Are we the only one to bear all the pain and suffering in this world? Where we lacked? We did everything and everything for him. Are you listening? I want the answers just give me the answers" I shouted.

I kneeled down and joined hands in front of the statue. I cried and cried. "I have never asked you for anything in my life before but today please hear my prayer. Please Please Bhavya ko theek kr do. Do some magic?"

One of the Gurudwara caretakers saw me and took me aside because I was blocking the way. I sat there until it was finally time to close the doors.

I met Shantanu later after his dinner. I hugged him tight. Still I could not stop. I wept on his shoulder.

"What happened? Why are you crying?" I just cried and cried. "First stop crying and tell me what happened?"

"Bhavya. . .Doctor said" I could not complete the sentence.

"Kya hua? What they said?"

"Mar jayega" I said weeping.

He said nothing rather held me tighter than before. After a couple of minutes we separated. He wiped his eyes. He loved Bhavya as much as I did.

I narrated him what all happened in the day.

I went to bed early that day.

Chapter 13

The God's Call

My mom compelled me to go the school the other day. There was nothing to do and if I sit at home my whole mind would be diverged there. I didn't tell anyone about Bhavya in the school. Only Raj knew about the reports last night.

When the clock showed time when I was suppose to reach home, I decided to inform mom about the one hour extra class. I took Raj's phone and went to a safe place where nobody could see me using a phone in the school premises.

I dialed her number. The bell rang for a minute but there was no response. I called again but again the same story.

I hung and switched on to the landline number. After a long bell "Hello" said an unfamiliar voice. For a second I thought I dialed a wrong number but before reverting back I checked it.

"Hello Ujjawal here. Mummy se baat kra do please? She was on the phone within a minute, in the respite I heard crowd murmuring in the background. "Mummy I'll be late by a hour."

"Okay. Listen Bhavya ki death ho gyi h" {Bhavya passed away}. I almost froze there when my left ear heard what she said.

"Shit kab?" I exploded.

"Today at 9:30 in the morning"

"I am coming home" I hung up.

I crossed the speed limit. I don't know why I wanted to reach home so quickly even though Bhavya was in Delhi. To the last turn for my house my bike slid in the mud. I had minor cuts on my legs and arms.

I showed my presence to the people who came to pay their sympathies and then went inside my room. I locked it from inside so that nobody could disturb me.

I sat with his photographs and videos. Recalled times spent with him. It made me smile and forgot that he is no more in this world. I closed my eyes and saw him and when I opened it he was gone. If he loves me in my dreams, don't wake me up then. I yearned for closing my eyes forever.

I lost my greatest source of happiness, someone who was irreplaceable, and someone who was my best teacher till date and he remains to be the one. As a child he taught me everything that my life did. Ultimately he was my life. I missed how when he wanted to hug me, I kneeled down and hugged him with all my strength like I will never let my toy break.

Now there is no one who would force me to buy a chocolate for him and walk with me hand in hand to the chocolate shop every evening. It is his voice that hallucinate "Ujju bhaiya". This voice is the only thing in the world that forces me to get up again. Nobody in the world gave me so much happiness, which I found when he was around. It is beyond words.

All these months I waited for him and he didn't arrive, death took him. I think God loved him more than I did, that's why he left me and went to the almighty. Such a mean he was. Things and people change suddenly isn't it?

You sure did leave me but I have your memories with me. You ditched me for death, right? Now look how I'll ditch life for you.

For me his last smile became eternal. His memories are now a treasure. The treasure hidden deep inside the heart that nobody in the coming years would be able to dig them out. My memories with him were sealed for Eternity.

When I got up from a small nap I came to know that his funeral is done in Delhi. I thought his cadaver would be brought here first because it was his last wish. He wanted to get back home. The hope of seeing him again broke down.

The whole day Raj, Kiarra, Summer and Shantanu called me to see if I was doing fine or not. Shantanu and Raj even came home in the evening.

Shantanu was available all throughout the day when I wanted him. He would leave his studies and come to me. Raj helped me with the school work.

In the night I saw Mahima gazing at the stars with crystals in her eyes. "For what?" I asked. She said, "I am searching for a new star. They say that dead become stars, I am searching for Bhavya." She continued after a pause, "The stars are too many. I guess I am not the only one with a dead family member then", the scattered bits of sadness were filled up to the edge.

I wept that night alone. I wished I could die before the sun rises. All seemed unreal like a nightmare.

Summer talked to me on the phone and comforted me.

Life gave me my best friends that day. These were worth more than hundred friends in my life. They made me believe that this darkest night of my life would end and the brightest sun would rise again.

<u>After a week</u>

I reached the railway station with my dad.

They came back with one less.

Dadi hugged me tight and cried. It reminded me of the time when my grandpa left us.

We kept a dinner at home in his name that day. Many relatives came home to enquire about Bhavya and offered their sympathies and condolences.

In the night when everything was at peace my father had a call from our far-flung relatives. I was in his room while he was busy on the phone.

I heard the whole story once again which I had been listening all throughout several days either from his mouth or any of our family member.

But this time he added a different fact, "The operation had only two end results either the patient would be cured or the patient would die."

The last line made my blood boil. It means that they lied to us?

When he hung up the phone I gathered all my courage to ask him a question but somehow I stopped myself.

But then when those lines kept on revolving in my mind I took out the matter. "Papa did you lie? I mean yes you did" my eyes became watery before I finished "But why?" I concluded.

"What I didn't get you?" he said in bewilderment.

"I heard your conversation very well dad. How dare you hide this fact from us? Bhavya was equal to one and all here. I loved him more than you."

He gave a sudden scared look, looked uncomfortable. He understood what I was pointing at but then he reacted that he didn't get what I asked him.

"You lied that Bhavya either will be cured or else will not. You never said that he will die once the operation is ineffective". My voice rose with every word. "Why? Why you did this? Bhavya meant everything to me. Are you listening?"

For the first time in my life I raised my voice in front of him. I was never this rude to him in my life before. He stood there in silence. I waited for his answer.

"We did this for Bhavya's own good. We didn't like to see him in a situation when he has to get syringes every month. I didn't want him to bear the pain and then cry. His one drop of tear made me sink." He said while stealing eyes from me.

"And now you would never see him again dad. He died crying. I saw the pain in his eyes when I met him. He was cursing us. What would have been his final thoughts when he closed his eyes forever? Can you think and feel what he must have felt? He would curse us when he gets to the heaven for we made his life so painful in the end. He would have appreciated if he would have died normally. For once if you had told me the real consequences I would have never let him go."

Mom was standing on the door. She heard all this too.

Before I could utter out a word more she came near me and slapped me. Her ring in the finger gave me a swell near the lips instantly. I fumbled backwards and lost my hearing for a second. I left the room and closed the door hard at their face.

I never have thought that my own family members would be like this. It was a breach of trust. My uncle was equally responsible. I decided to keep a distance from him.

Chapter 14

The Warmth

I uploaded a picture with her a day back. It was young, happy, classy, natural, freeze and then there was she. It was the best photo that I ever had with her.

'You are the chosen one <3' it read on the screen with the photo. I said I Love You in a different manner that day. Although I told her everyday but I don't know whether she hears it or not? Sometimes it was hard to find words to tell her how much she meant to me.

"Ujjawal we are dead now. The people will kill us in the school tomorrow. Anyway you are the best <3 :* :')" That was her first reaction on the photo.

Then she commented 'Ujjawal <3 you look perfect'.

My best friends had also left their comment on my cover picture and it was their first time in all these years.

I put it as my mobile screen wallpaper, every time I looked up in my mobile I saw her. I was secretly falling for her in those days.

In the school people congratulated me on my new girlfriend. I wanted to hug them for their kind gesture, but wait I had been telling them for years that she is not my girlfriend and I was saying the same thing again and again. I had nothing to prove my statement; all the things were against me. After all this was all because of me. Taking walks in the school, updating pictures with such captions and hanging out with her could have created an understanding of me and her in anybody's mind.

The half yearly examination was a head ache.

What happened in the previous days did not help me to concentrate into my studies. Then there was she. Every time I tried to study, her message unsettled me from books.

I deposited my phone with mom to stay away from her and not repeat history. I buried myself into the books as much I could.

I noticed after some days a puppy on the roads near our house. The dog was pale, lacking energy and starving; searching for life. I didn't pay much attention until on a rainy day I saw that dog near the chambers shivering and losing life. Not until I had seen this dog starving nobody had helped him under the circumstances. Apparently his mother was not there to take his care, the dog was all alone.

I and my mom took him inside the shed that day. We started feeding that dog with some bread and milk, biscuits etc from that time. I never ignored him. He chases me and makes me march towards the Kirana shop for a packet of Parle-G biscuit every day. When I am bored I take my football out and make him run behind it, we play together.

This dog reminds me of Bhavya. I feed him like he is my own lost brother and play with him like I played with my one lost part of the soul. It was an unseen and unsaid connection.

The atmosphere at home started to settle down. Things started becoming the same as they were before but one thing didn't change from that night. I didn't exchange a word with my dad although he tried a couple of times. To not to talk to him I avoided his company as much as I could.

By the end of the month the Navratri had started. Kiarra went everyday to play Garba in one of the societies. She would reserve passes for me hoping I would come and watch her Garba someday but my mom never allowed me to go because of my exams.

On the last day of the festival I went to see her performance. For my company I took Raj along with me. I saw her. As usual she looked best in traditional dress. The Ghaghra {Garba dress} was made for her. She looked incredible.

We entered with the pass which she had reserved for me for so long. We clicked photos until her turn came.

In the crowd my eyes only looked for her. They did that in a circle so she was visible from my side for a minute and then she would disappear. Not every time my eyes met with her but for once when it did for a long time I winked at her and she forgot her steps. That was a funny moment. When she came back she scolded me for it. I loved it when she did that.

After she was done with her Garba we both went for a walk. We had left Raj and Kavya along with their friends in the food court.

It was 12 on the clock and I was surprised my parents had not asked me where I was and what I was doing so late? I was happy they didn't care. It was liberation beyond possible expectations.

We walked down the empty lane. Everything was at peace and this was the type of scene I wanted with her. A dog crossed by her side and she held my hand for a second. It took me by surprise. She then removed it quickly.

It reminded me of Bhavya when he used to walk with me hand in hand in the garden. His and Her hand gave me all the happiness of the world.

I decided to take that hand. She had accepted my relationship with her already and I was still confused to choose between 12th boards and her. Decide one my heart softly whispered.

My mind asked a millions question which my heart didn't wished to answer.

I decided to propose her that time. The time was right, the place was right and the two hearts were precise.

That time I had nothing with me, any chocolate or flowers. I plucked a flower from a patch of shrubs in front of a house. Its fragrance was fresh. She didn't get what I was up to.

I felt a bit nervous as I moved towards her. Without a second thought about my 12th boards I took her right hand and kneeled down, in the middle of the empty road. And as I kneeled on the ground it was an 'Aww' moment for her.

"Kiarra I Love you. Be my Girlfriend?" Her lips smiled and eyes twinkled.

"Have I ever said no to anything you have asked for?" What I heard was riddling, what I saw was more beautiful than anything in the world, what I felt happened without any Rhyme or Reason. The reply was indirectly direct but my senses gave me a blank understanding. Only Heart knew it was love.

I took her another hand and pulled her down. We both stared into each other's eyes. Her eyes were filled with stars of joy.

My knees pained by the rough base. Nothing happened when she said "what?"

"What?" I replied back.

She leaped on me. I felt the sweet fragrance of her and the world was in my clutch. Her hug set my broken pieces back again.

"I will never leave your hand no matter what happens. I love you so damn very much Kiarra. Stay forever please." I hugged her tight.

"I will and you know what I love you more than you do."

We separated because my phone rang. It was my dad's call. I didn't pick up. We walked hand in hand for a couple of minutes until I was again interrupted by a call. This time my mom called.

"Haan bolo" I replied.

"Kaha h tu? Jaldi ghr a papa ghussa ho rhe h" her voice conveyed she was fuming too. I wanted to stay with her. I wish the whole night was ours.

"Kiarra I had to leave now it's time."

"Yeah okay, my parents should be waiting too." She clasped me to her bosom before leaving.

We decided not tell about our relationship to anybody in the school. Telling them or not telling them would mean the same thing now.

On the way home I told Raj that I proposed her and as soon I blurt that out of my mouth he stopped the bike, got down and pulled me up by collar.

"Have you gone mad? You get your brain on track okay?" He put his hands in frustration on his head. "You are finished, your life is over, you are gone I am telling you. Your pocket money is not yours now; half of the money will go into recharge and the rest to fill her stomach. Who will fill my? Life also gives you a second chance bro relationship would not give you one chance. You are going to cry a lot I am telling you. Over man your life is over. I'm going to miss you bro."

"Dude, at this point I must mention the best thing is that I don't have to be in relationship with my hand anymore. No more acne and pimples." I looked at my red pizza like face in the side mirror, crying deep from inside.

I am really going to ask her, if she would help me lose my virginity. I really thought about it when she said yes, (when I proposed her) and I was like the day would come soon" I said smiling widely at him.

He looked at me as he was already looking but this time with his wide eyes open and before I could make sense of what he thought about relationship, he showed me a middle finger, such a feminist. I know he was just jealous; he wanted to be in a relationship too and have some sex.

"Fine" I conceded.

Billion girls in this world but my heart chose her.

I was stuck in the biggest gamble of life. Two best friends were in a relationship now.

Chapter 15

Kiarra

I was ten minutes late because of the traffic. She was waiting for me outside the Gurudwara. I apologised to her with a rose.

"Aww it is so cute; thank you Ujjawal. It wasn't needed actually. You came that is enough for me." She smelled it and then held it firmly in her wrist. We took a walk. I held those soft hands again to make her feel safe and loved.

Like this I wanted her to walk with me all throughout my life. I want her to stay with me when my life goes from up to down, from a smile to a frown, from happy to sad.

We sat on the service road. Nobody used that road because it was under construction so we didn't fear that any vehicle would come and knock us both down.

Time passed quickly and the sun started to disappear behind the skyline. She kept me busy in the conversation. Never before she had talked to me like this. Discussing things and scolding me in Love for my small mistakes and carelessness, and in her anger I saw her undying care. She opened her heart to me. She would tell me about the dress she wanted to buy, shade of nail polish, subject she hated, her favourite dish, what kind of books she likes to read and at the end of it how much she loved me. It is silly how I too started sharing each and every part of my life with her. I won her trust in these days.

It was difficult to stop her when she was in the flow. I was wondering where I went so right. I choose her, meaning I choose her smile moreover her life. Her doodles and her cute face, Oh My God! Beautiful, it is my worst distraction.

She didn't even know what she was saying and kept on floating like a cloud under the sky. I kept on listening as if she was giving the answer to the questions of my life.

To stop her I moved forward to kiss her in between but she pushed me with her hands. "No ladies first" She said.

She moved towards me and whispered "No" in my ears. I thought she would kiss me on the cheek.

"You are not doing it and you are not letting me to do it. Then what do you want?" I asked. And when I went for her cheeks again she got up and ran. At first I didn't get up. I asked her to come and sit but she challenged me to get her till she reaches the Gurudwara gates.

She ran on the muddy road. I was scared and hoped that she doesn't slip, so I didn't chase her. I didn't care for the kiss but I cared for her more.

After she safely reached there I ran towards her. She teased me that I couldn't catch her. I lost to her but for me I was the winner.

"You can kiss me now" She said in the same sentiment in which I asked. I refused her proposal to make her feel what I felt when she refused.

In My Eternity

She said "Let me complete the whole sentence. I was saying that, first write a love letter to me and then take as many kisses as you wish to." Girls are smarter aren't they?

If she had asked me to I would have turn around the world for her, writing a love letter was nothing. I accepted it whole-heartedly.

She called her driver who had parked the car on some distance from the Gurudwara. I hugged her before her driver came.

I got home and the till midnight wrote my Business studies assignment. When I was busy I concentrated on my work and when I paused she was in my mind.

I started to leave for the school a bit early from those days so that I could reach school along with her bus. The best part of the story was that her class and my class were opposite to each other. After every period we both come out to have a glance at each other.

Things had really changed in the last few days. I loved going to school now. I didn't hesitate to get up in the morning and go to school because there I see her after a long wait. I have changed my routes to the class just to catch a glimpse of her.

One day during the recess we met.

It was the only path where she had proposed me earlier and I was waiting for her to say or tell me something more beautiful this time, but today she had altogether a different story.

"Ujjawal, you know what yesterday Kavya told everybody in our group that we are committed now. It was my fault only that I didn't tell her that she should not tell anybody that we both are committed and yesterday in the night at two Vedant called me. He shouted at me so badly and I cried."

Kavya's mistake was accepted but what Vedant did was not good.

"He's gone now. I'll make him pay for what he has done and how dare he make you cry. You just wait and watch." My anger rose.

I never thought love was worth fighting for but if it involved her I was ready for the war.

"No don't do anything. I have talked to him last night and cleared out everything. The best thing is he is not talking to me now."

"But why? I always want to get involve in fight with that devil and it's such a perfect time."

"Promise me you will never get into a fight with him? And leave him he is such an asshole."

"Okay promise."

"What about the letter. How is it going?"

"Umm I have not yet started it."

"You want the kiss or not"

"YES" I said on a high note.

"Then write it soon. And yes I am going out of town with family and would be back in three days after that we'll meet. I want the letter then" she demanded.

"Don't you think I want the kiss more than you want the letter?"

She laughed. I swear I can't even blink my eyes when she did every time.

I sat down to write the letter a day before when she would come to school. I had a blank sheet of paper to fill in front of me. I thought what to write for the next half an hour but could not pen down anything. I tore three sheets of paper already.

How easily I presumed, I can turn around the world for her and here I was struggling with the letter.

I took help of my dad; indirectly. I remembered mom telling me that my father used to write letters to her before they married. I asked mom to give me those letters. Before I could get them I struggled hard to tell her why I wanted them.

I had collected a lot of material and concepts through those letters and internet. Everything, the sentences and the words depicted our romance. I sat down to mix the words into story before they slip down my mind.

My pen never realised, what was pouring down wasn't just ink. I poured my heart out with my pen.

Raj came home that day to take my notebook to complete his incomplete work. I showed him this letter. I told him the why I wrote a letter for her. He found it fanatical.

"Kiss her on the forehead first. Girls feel good when a boy kisses them there." He advised. Even though he was single, but he had been advising me to do this and to do that to make her feel special from the day I was tied with her.

I was so amazed to see how beautiful Love was in the beginning and was waiting to see how beautiful it could get further.

. . .

'Hey Kiarra it was tough finding words for you but here I have something for you. Though I am late but I think I have the perfect girl now and I know boys out there would be jealous of me.

There was a time when I didn't know your name but today that's the only word that is on my tongue every time. Kiarra I love you so much. I love you the way you are. My Love for you is so deep that you cannot imagine.;)

No girl has ever made me feel the way you do. Missing you has become a hobby these days. When I am with you I am just happy for no reason.

I stop and stand for a while when my eyes see you. I like your smile. It gives me unexplained happiness every time. Perhaps this is when all of me loves all of you, love your curves and all your edges, all your perfect imperfections.

Sometimes I wish I would write I miss you on a stone and then throw at you and when it will hurt you then you will understand how much I get hurt when you don't miss me.

I don't have a crush on you I love you. I hope you can understand the difference. Just love me and never leave me never, I want to grow old with you my love. I don't know whether I will love you always or forever because I don't know which is longer, but I promise I will love you till day tom finally eats jerry, the day when sun would rise from the west, the day when an apple would fall from a mango tree.

You love me to the moon and back right. Tell you I love you to the Pluto and back. I love you and that's the beginning and the end of everything between us. I wish to die in your Arms.

Stay forever.

Your crazy boyfriend- Ujjawal <3'

She read the letter making her pony tail with hands above and I bet she looked a trillion times more jaw drop gorgeous. As soon she did she cuddled me and I did what Raj advice me to do.

Thunder boomed in the clouds and then lights flashed. Suddenly the atmosphere changed. The dark clouds covered the earth. The sharp winds blew passed by the skin. It gave a shiver. Piles of leaves covered the path. The leaves stirred along the path hopelessly finding life which was no more. Vibrant colour of red, yellow and orange flowers lay pressed on the path. It was dusk by then and the mothers chirped on the branches of the tree to call their children home.

The sky was black and a loving fragrance came from the Earth. It was subtle. Heavy rain storm was about to hit the earth.

We ordered coffee. She read the letter again and again. I tried to talk but she was buried in her own story.

Meanwhile I looked up in the dark sky from the window recalling times of my childhood. How I eagerly waited for the rains to stop so that after it I could have some best childhood days with my mates.

Though I had an unexplained fear of heavy rains but the best part came when it will stop. Our residential area didn't have the best of drainage system and every time a bit of rains would fill the drenches.

Krishh and I would then go on the streets with old newspapers. We would call our other friends too.

Everybody would gather at one place and would make their paper boats. We would decorate it with colour markers so as to differentiate ours from the others. After everyone was prepared with their boats we would set for their sail then in the biggest puddle. Everybody would try hard by blowing air from their mouth to take their boat to the destination.

These boat races were an exciting adventure.

And then as we grew even more we changed our game. We would take our cycles and play Police thief in and after the rains. Splashing muddy water by the cycle tyre was the favourite thing to do.

We would fall trying to catch each other on the cycle. We got hurt but in the end it was all fun that we had. After such fun everyone would get a beating from their mother.

And with advancing age these games became uninteresting. We switched games frequently.

From then till this time we play street soccer in the rains.

I missed those friendship days while living in my love ones.

The rain poured from the Heaven and the waiter came with the coffee. Nothing bothered her. I snatched the paper from her. It tore a bit.

"Arre give me" she said.

"Coffee first." I pointed at the glass between us.

In My Eternity

We shared a single straw. I sipped slowly as I wanted to spend more time, talk more and share more with her. The sound of the rain contributed music to the ears.

"Let's go for a walk" she demanded.

"We'll get wet" I gave an excuse. I never told her that I was scared of the heavy rain.

"It will be fun. Come on." I said nothing. She held my wrist and pulled me out of the Cafeteria. I felt the silver water droplets over my head. I felt the breeze kissing my face.

We rambled down the empty road.

I held her hand tight as I was afraid. She held it even tighter.

Hard rains and hands were pulling each other closer.

We walked and walked. The rain never stopped nor I wanted it to. For the first time I loved rain. I drowned with her in its music.

We danced in the rain as if nobody saw. We both splashed water and ran behind each other.

I held her in my hands. For a minute we stared and then she smiled looking at me. I blew her lips and her voice echoed in my heart. I got wet twice, first from the rain and then from her lips. The rain continued behind.

It made the moment. It was autumn's best cheer. And there was an all-pervading feeling. The sun broke from the clouds and we held aback. It ceased the moment. It was all quite again.

The walk revealed some extraordinary things. I loved rain now. I could now say 'bring it now' with no fear. I was thankful to her for such things.

I got home and I got a scolding from mom. She was chastising me for no reason. When I asked her to come to the point she bowled me clean. "Who is Kiarra?"

She stared for a minute or two with her hand on the waist and I stood smiling at her. I was expecting a chappal thrash at me. Chappals earlier deployed me from a naughty boy in my childhood.

"Let papa come. I'll tell him everything."

"Tell him I don't care."

"Ahahahan Ujjawal is in love LOL." Krishh scoffed at me as he entered the room. I had already told him about her.

I was busy in my room completing my assignment after dinner when papa called me. At first I did pay heed to what he said but at the second call I went to his room.

"So you broke your rule number one also." So the words have reached him, I was taken aback. I was expecting a smack at me anytime for being involved in the nonsense. I was scared. I gave a not understanding expression.

"Who's the lucky girl?" he said amiably.

I felt hesitated in responding to him. What happened after that night I have not been so frank and friendly with him. Mummy and Krishh kept staring at me. I felt awkward.

"I am sorry dad. I I. . . am sorry for being so rude to you. I know how it feels. Please I am sorry."

"Come and sit here. It is absolutely fine. It happens (happens what? Love?), there have been times where I also was rude to my father and I have realised its worth too. Forget everything."

In My Eternity

He took his hand forward like children do when they want to patch up for their friendship again. It felt a bit absurd but then he was kind and how can be rude to him? I put my right hand forward and we shook hands.

"Btw her name is Kiarra. It's complete two weeks today." I said.

"Only then I was wondering from so many days. I knew there is something. I saw you smiling a lot of times when you look at your phone. Anyway enjoy but be in control don't you know get into those things."

"Haha sure dad"

"Instead of telling him to stay away from her you are driving him." My mom exploded.

"Mom! Papa has said what he wanted to and now nothing can change. Good night and thanks dad." I gave a Hi-fi to him.

I completed my work and then I called Kiarra. My routine shifted. I started sleeping at around 2'o clock every day.

Eye lids became heavier with every message. Ultimately all the serious talks were done in the night. Even after a bye we talked for an hour more. Nobody wanted to see the next day.

The Deepawali break was on. There was no cherishment or keenness this time among us. We missed Bhavya like anything. To remove the frustration I decided to ask her for a day out for the evening.

I picked up my phone and saw there was already a message from her.

'Guess what?'

'What? Don't you say you want a letter again.'

'Haha I will. I am with Nakul right now.' A sudden pain, it took me by surprise. What is she doing with her ex? I knew Nakul already. He is my mummy's best friend's son.

I called her that moment. I called five times but not a single time she picked up my phone. I was jealous and this little jealousy was nice to know that I was afraid of losing her.

'What are you doing with him and pick my call at once.' I messaged her. 'Kiarra?'

I called Kavya. She told she is not with her and doesn't know her whereabouts.

I called Nakul then. He didn't pick up my call too. It concerned me a bit. I have never trusted Nakul in my life. He cheated with his other friends when it comes to girls and I think he is on to me but I realised I have certainly not told him that I am in relationship with Kiarra.

Perhaps Kiarra must have.

I started feeling that something was going wrong.

I went with mom for some Diwali Shopping. All throughout my attention was on the phone. For the next couple of hours there was no call or text from her side and I was thinking about her like crazy. My notification bar was empty.

I called her again when I reached home. She picked it this time.

"Where were you both? I dropped a several messages and called so many times, where is your phone? Don't you think answering me is your first job rather than wandering with your ex and that too without asking me?"

"Ujjawal calm down. Calm down. I can totally understand. Listen what happened was Nakul invited me for lunch."

"It means that you both dated each other right."

"No, we had a bet and he lost so that is why he gave a treat. I am sorry my phone was on silent and I had kept it in the purse that is why I was not able to take your call."

I felt like whatever she said was false. But then in these days she had not lied to me a single time, I trusted her completely.

"Okay. Anyway are you meeting me tomorrow?"

"I am sorry I won't be able to. I have to go shopping with my mom."

"Okay let it be we'll plan some other day"

"I am free the day after Deepawali. Let's go for a movie."

"Sure. I got to go I am sorry bye. I love you"

"Bye Ujji I love you toooooo"

I hung up the phone. Next I called Nakul. I cut the phone before the bell rang.

But why am I doing this? I should trust her. Still I called him. I wanted to cross check whether whatever she said was true or not.

We both fixed up a meeting soon.

Chapter 16

Chaos!

I cooled down a bit from what happened a day before. I had a long three hour phone call with her last night.

Nevertheless I went to Nakul's residence the other day. He welcomed me with a warm hug. My temper for him calmed down a bit in a day and for his humble approach towards me I did not feel like cross checking anything.

We talked about the normal things at first and then I took out her topic. "You met Kiarra recently?" I questioned. I noted hesitations on his face.

"Yes only two days ago. You two have anything? Your cover photo and all."

"Hahaha no she is a best friend that's it. Why met her?"

"Jealousy! I see. Why do I tell you?"

"So now you are hiding anything from me it seems?" I asked him at length. He glanced down on the floor, looked baffled.

"Everything" He looked up and laughed belligerently. "Okay I am telling you this because you are my trustable friend. Don't tell anyone, not even her."

"Yeah I'll better protect it."

In My Eternity

"The day before my date with her I called her in the night. We talked for some hours. We both planned to meet and the purpose was that I wanted to kiss her. My relationship with her lasted for only a week and in that I did nothing. So I thought why not now. I asked her whether she will. She said she still hold some feeling for me. I booked the movie tickets for the next day's show in the morning and took two corner seats so that I can play the game."

I certainly didn't show how I felt but it was like a hit with a bullet straight in the place where she was. I just wanted to smack him in his face. How do I blame him, how do I tell him that she is my girlfriend? I forget about her that moment. My ears were pleading to hear what happened next.

"So you did. Did you?"

"No we missed the movie. She was late. Then we went to the restaurant because I had to give her a treat also."

"Bad luck, all the best for next time."

"Never mind dude she is an ugly ass. There are so many hot chicks around. I'll catch them. I won't call her next time."

If I had stayed a minute more there I would have got involved in the fight. I left by giving an excuse.

I walked with 1000 questions in my mind towards home. I took the long path so that I can think even more on what happened.

Whom to judge right and wrong? I think the answer was clearly in front of me but I was not ready to accept it.

Whatever she said to me on the phone was right but she never told me about the movie. Why would she?

On the morning of Deepawali I called to greet her but she didn't pick up my phone. I messaged her 'Happy Diwali.' For 3 hours there was no reply.

I called her again but this time too she didn't care to answer my call. I messaged her at facebook, I called her from a different number, I called Kavya and I did everything to get to her but no response.

This year's Deepawali was totally spoiled. We didn't burn any crackers because of Bhavya's demise.

A conversation from her side would have set everything straight.

After one complete week I had her response from a different number.

'Ujjawal I am really sorry. I miss you so much. I will tell you what all happened. Actually mom came to know about you and me. She read our messages and then she was going to tell dad but somehow I controlled. I know I am disappointing you for so many days. Try and understand dad also checked my phone bill details. He even asked about the 500+ messages I sent to your number and he had stopped my phone services. I am missing you like hell Ujjawal I want to meet you tomorrow and yeah 'Happy one month Anniversary Love <3 :*'.

It means that Nakul has not told her anything.

I called Raj and told him about the message. "Are you a fool sitting here accepting her replies? End things now I just can't take it anymore" Raj admitted.

"She had not kissed Nakul. I can clear out things and make her understand that things are not so straight in love. I don't want to lose her. I will meet her. Make her understand. If she does understand me fine if not no worries at all after all she cheated on me."

He did not agree with my decision.

"As you stand here, defending her, mind you she is going to betray you further. Things are clear Ujjawal; care about moving further rather than to her." He shouted at me for letting her go for what she had done. For he had not trusted her from the beginning, he even warned me before.

Later after thinking too much I wrote what I wanted to but then I backspaced.

I messaged her "Happy one month Anniversary It's okay no worries. You meet me first then tell me the whole thing I miss you to baby."

"It's our first, a table for four." I booked the table for the evening as I got up from bed in the morning.

We met to celebrate one month of our togetherness. She gave me a warm hug. I could feel her wet hair on my cheek. Covered around her arms gave me a safe and sound feeling as if nothing had happened.

"Kiarra Happy one month Anniversary"

"Same to you. I Love you so much"

We took the table. She was surprised to see a bouquet of red roses, a cake and a love letter. I ordered to put all these at my table before she come.

"Awww Ujjawal you do so much for me. I Love you I love you I love youuuuuu."

"Shut up this is nothing. I can do anything for you." She took my right hand and kissed it.

"Sorry I didn't bring anything for you."

"Have I ever asked for anything from you? You are back that's enough for me."

"I never left Ujjawal."

"Anyway let's celebrate."

"Wait any more surprises? " She asked with a bit of luck.

"If you want I can bring them right now."

"Will you?" She was excited than before.

"As I said I can do anything for you. You just got to order me."

"Okay then where is my next surprise?"

"Wait" I texted someone on the phone while she kept looking at me.

"Let's cut the cake. Your surprise is almost there."

As we went for the cake Raj and Kavya clapped and sang the song. She turned back. She left the chair.

For her it was an 'Aww' moment again. She hugged Kavya. They both had arrived with me.

"This is your surprise. Thanks for coming dude and you to Kavya."

"Arre my Jiju invited me and how can I deny?" We all four laughed.

We both cut the cake together.

In My Eternity

We spent some hours on the table bantering.

"Happy Journey you two. Enjoy." I said and bid them goodbye.

She came near me and kissed me. "Thank you for everything."
They both then left.

I was happy. My whole 1500 Rs surprise was worth it. Buying
a gift for her and then giving all of them a treat required days
of planning. I had to flatter my dad, run errands for my mom
and saved a bit of my pocket money for the whole expenses
incurred.

The thing I wanted to cross check still remained an unanswered
question. Somewhere deep inside the thought killed me. After
such a beautiful time with her that evening I decided to kill
the thought and next time kill me if I ever think of something
like that.

The thoughts would often rise on but my voice never did.
Somewhere I could smell the betrayal still.

A day without her in the school was boring and I had 5 days
more to spend without her. She was on her Australia Tour from
the school. She had requested and pleaded me to join in for the
trip but I knew what I was going through at home.

Me: 'Kiarra listen remember I told you about the basketball
match? Guess what we won and we are in the
finals now.'

Kiarra: 'My mood is off Ujjawal we'll talk later☺.' This line
worried me for once she had told me that I am the
only one whom she wishes to talk when she is upset.
It made me questioning why she does not want to talk

to me. I understood there was something unwonted related to me.

Kiarra: 'Need to talk to you.' She again messaged me after sometime.

Me: 'Hey? Yes what?'

Kiarra: 'What did you say to Vinni?'

Me: 'Yes we had a chat after the classes were over. Why?'

Kiarra: 'What did you say?'

Me: 'Nothing much she asked me about today's Basketball match that's it.'

Kiarra: 'No anything about me.'

Me: 'No Kiarra, I never talk about you in front of any girl. Yeah one or two times she took out your topic but then I ignored.

Did she talk about our relationship?'

Kiarra: 'I am not talking of today. Anything before?'

Me: 'No Kiarra, I swear to god.'

Kiarra: 'You know what she said? She said that you told her that 'You don't like me but you proposed because I pleaded so many times that is why. . .'

Me: 'You got to believe me I never said this kind of shit. And tell you first thing that she is the one who want us both to breakup.'

Kiarra: 'Your friend has said it how I cannot believe the fact.'

Ujjawal: 'Damn what the hell? I am saying you why don't you believe me?'

Kiarra: 'Will talk to you later. NEVERMIND!'

Ujjawal: 'See if you trust me a bit meet me in the school when you come and then will talk what all happened. Goodbye and have a safe trip.'

Next day in the school, I thought of having a word with Vinni but I didn't.

We five stood in the middle of the court. Our strength was as 5 fingers combined. We were ready to punch the opposite team. Sathya Sai School was in final of a Basketball tournament after ages and we were urging to bring trophy at home.

Chief Guest came to shake hands with the Basketball finalists. I as the captain of the team introduced ma'am with the rest four. She then moved towards the opponent team.

Our opponents had 3 Indian Camp players and we five have never touched the state rounds.

We did some stretching and shooting. We went to our coach. He assigned our man to us. When the game plan was revised he took the ball in his hand and put it between us. We all put hands at the ball. "Bajrang Bali ki" he said. "Jay" All continued.

My heart pumped the rhythm of unity. We were not scared.

I had number 2 behind my back and I had taken it purposely. It was her Birthday date.

Aman the Michael Jordan of the team did the Jump ball. Unluckily he could not collect it. I took my man and instructed others too. They attacked in the first minute of the game. It was a three pointer.

The first quarter was over and we were nine down. What we could make out of the first quarter was that their attack was fast and their defence was not easy to break. Our coach instructed us to play zone instead of man-marking and to play more one to one game.

With hopes to play better and not to repeat any flaws again we entered the court. This time we were both efficient and effective. We mostly covered their nine down lead to 8-9. Ultimately we had not let them score a basket in the second quarter. Our first basket came from Kabir and there was cheer at every basket and claps at their miss. They kept us motivated into the game.

In the third quarter we were a bit exhausted. We had no option for substitution as we five on the court were the only one, rest on the benches were taken to fill the team and get ourselves registered into the tournament.

The point lead changed every minute. At times they lead the game and we tried covering the lead. It was difficult to maintain the body balance along with game. I requested sir for a time out. The rest of the boys prepared glucose for us. It was really warm under the bright sun.

In My Eternity

With the approaching end towards the quarter with decided to attack. I succeeded at the first attempt but it was a violation and hence was not counted. Sir shouted at me for it. The whole we time attacked when the ball was in their half and defended when it was in our half. We assigned Mridul and Kabir to take shots while I focused on the rebound. I had the best jump in the whole team.

With growing frustration of not getting points one of the opponent players fouled Mridul while he was attempting a shot. Raj exchanged some fowl words with the player. Two free shots were awarded.

Ultimately Rishabh had to sit down he had a back injury and was not able to continue.

We began the last quarter with a lead of 4 points. The score board showed 20-16. Now we had to protect that lead in any case. The coach of the opponent team threw a trump card in the last quarter. All five faces were changed. This created problem. Our game strategy for the last quarter became ineffective. The major drawback was that Mridul was sitting on the bench. The problem grew even more when Raj reached the maximum fowl limits. With every fowl of his the opponent team would be given free two points. We moved him from defense to attack.

The scorecard didn't changed until Raj committed another fowl. The lead reduced down to two points. We defended in the last moment to protect it.

But they ended as they began. In the eleventh hour of the game one of the tiny tit from their gang hit a three pointer and then everything was over. We lost 20-21.

We accepted the loss. We all shook hands with our opponents. Had Raj not committed any foul and Mridul did not have to sit back we could have won the match and hearts of many too.

It was hell of a game. All throughout there was suspense. We lost maybe because we entered the court with an aim to defeat them but they played to clinch the trophy.

The game was one of the memory to be taken back when I'll leave school ultimately nobody remembers who came second.

. . .

Before leaving home I decided that, if she is going to talk to me about the matter well and good and if not I will leave her all alone. In the school I waited for the recess. Meanwhile during lectures I practiced my lines.

I waited at the basketball court for her to come. After a while I saw them. They didn't approach me rather sat on the staircase to the classrooms.

It raised my heartbeat even more. I was scared to hear from her. I was just thinking where I had gone wrong. I never contacted the girl who said all these things, I know I was right I had never said anything like that to anybody but then what about those things which I didn't say about her. Where did it come from?

They showed blind face as I moved towards them. I concluded the situation there and then. I stopped in front of her and waited for her to greet me or say a Hi but she got up and moved. I stopped her.

"Kiarra what happened? Tell me." I asked.

She didn't respond. Not even her expression said anything. A dilemma presented itself, propounded.

"She doesn't want to talk to you. So please you go away" Kavya reconfirmed.

I quietly without a word moved towards my class. I did not enjoyed complications and hence I left.

I never knew I was involved in game of false hopes and hidden distrust. Was I ever important to her? What happened to our love? Where did it go? What about the promises she made? It was all like I am her forever boyfriend and she was my seldom girlfriend.

I decided to give her some time to think. If I hold any place in her heart she would come back and clear out things but I am not going to put a step forward. It was not ego but a matter of Self respect.

After seven days

Still there were stolen glances at each other. I can imagine how much a three letter word called 'ego' can completely destroy some relationships.

I was still waiting for her to call me or text me or talk to me either way. Though I convinced myself that I am not going to her but I still waited for her to do something that would change my mind. After giving her so many days to think about, she was not ready. I think she was not ready to continue.

I gave up on her. I decided to end this. It was one of the most difficult decisions for me to make. I wanted time to heal everything but maybe I was not ready to give life another chance.

'Well Kiarra you got to believe me I never said that shitty thing. Trust me. You know I was serious for you. Maybe I forgot the type of girl you are. My friends also told me not to get involve with you because you are not the kind of girl who would stay. They were true but I was mistaken. I misunderstood the fact. I drooled towards you.

Plus no doubt what do you thought I don't know about you. What are you doing, who are you meeting behind my back? I know the day when you and Nakul went together you and Nakul planned to kiss right? Hopefully you didn't. Shame on you! You know what I ignored the fact just because I was scared I would lose you but now it doesn't matter. I cared for you more than you think. Damn I don't know why I trusted you, why I cared so much? I know I was a fool. I don't know what Vinni told you. I don't know why you didn't come to me to clear things. Anyway all the best for your future Kiarra, I am done with you. Thank you for everything and then nothing.'

I typed these words on the screen and then pressed the enter key.

I had her reply on the next day.

Kiarra: Excuse me talk to me in front of Nakul. If you don't know anything you should tell these big things to any girl. And yeah the whole school told a lot what you told them about me. I didn't even ask you. I have proofs as well. I have screenshots. I was going to clear out things but this text. Nice! You are an amazing actor. You won't need any hard work later.

Enjoy with your 'popularity' your 'juniors' and your 'fan following.' Stay happy and do one thing for me. Until and unless you don't have any sureties about any girl don't say anything against her or don't spread any rumours. Okay? Goodbye.'

Well what she said hit me hard. I was clueless and I shouldn't have believed a person that he went to kiss my girlfriend.

Kiarra: Why would you care? Ujjawal I was attached to you a lot. I didn't expect anything like this from you. Anyway let's not fight Bye.

Me: Wait a sec. Do you trust me? And Why I will say anything against you?

Kiarra: I trusted you a lot. I was ready to forget everything because somewhere my heart didn't allowed me to believe that you can say anything about me but now not after what you have said never. Don't text now.

I talked to Summer on the phone that evening. She made me realised what I have said was wrong. She told me how I could have made certain things on track again. I realised that it was I who made things worse than ever. Those words were never from my heart, it was my anger that spoke off.

I should not have said anything like that to her. In the end she was ready to make things good but why I did that. Where my patience was? How do I tell her that it was my anger that spoke off my heart did not?

I thought of again cross checking it with Nakul and tell him that she is my girl friend and did he really. . .?

But it was no use of crying over the split milk. What meant to be has found its way. It was better for me to leave them both and not talk to them to make things worse.

One day Raj took to me to them in the recess. "Both of you clear out those things fast" he demanded.

"Oh hello please I don't want to clear anything okay." I moved from the scene. My heart was broken but love remained intact. Raj remained there for a couple of minutes and then came back.

"What is wrong with you? She wanted to talk to you and you?"

"Raj, please I don't want to clear out anything. I'm over it you get that?" I was resolute with my words.

In the evening he threw me at her again. He showed me some screenshots; it was his and Kiarra's chat.

{Kiarra: Raj Bhaiya I still believe in making everything fine soon. I know what Ujjawal said wasn't true. He cannot say anything like that to me. It was not the real he.

Raj: Kiarra I can understand. He was really frustrated about the Nakul thing. You don't worry I'll talk to him.}

I remained quiet to their talks.

Chapter 17

Are you happy?

My anger finally ripped off after few days and I started realizing that I am missing her. Whosoever I met, I talked about her. Once we did that. . . Kiarra and I. . . Kiarra this and Kiarra that. . . Our memories lasted longer.

Million times in a day I would think that I am over it, but then at the end of the day just a single 'no' was enough for me to deem I was not. Forgetting was hard for me as I had a heart for her.

I would read our chats often. Nothing was wrong but nothing was right either. I wanted to know the root cause of my breakup. I was inquisitive to know what actually happened from her side. But how do I do? I wanted someone's help for sure.

I called Raj for it.

"I tried to help you out but not now. And when you have decided to close the door why jumping out of the window then?" This was shaky for me.

Whenever I was in front of her I acted as I didn't bother about her. I wanted to show her that she doesn't concern me anymore. But it was all a sham. I don't know why I was faking things while being real needed no efforts.

147

I took shots someday. Believe me the glass of bear burned less than asking her that whatever she did was okay?

The news spread and with all possible haste that I broke up with her. My break up with her was not the only thing that troubled me but also the never ending comments. I was a bright student and did not enjoy any of the defamatory remarks.

'Let it be you deserve better' they say, I was fed hearing these words. Every next person whom I met said this. But who were they to question my choice?

I left the thing and then moved my mind towards the approaching examinations.

I contacted Nikita after my pre-boards were over. She was one of Kiarra's roommates during the Australia tour. They had become good friends on the trip.

As far as she could tell me she was not aware of any such things but yeah she told me that this Vinni was spreading rumours about me and Kiarra in the whole school. She wanted us to breakup because she had a serious crush on me and Kiarra too was aware of this.

Then why the hell she believed her? Why she did not trust me?

I spoke to Nikita more in order to gain my trust on her. I had told her not to tell Kiarra that I am in touch of her. When I was sure that I was able to trust her completely I threw the card.

I requested her to help me out with Kiarra. She agreed at one go. I prepared a self made chat. It seemed real but although it was not. I explained Nikita about the whole plan.

It was in the beginning of the day when I called Nikita to send me the message.

In My Eternity

Nikita: Hey wassupp. . .?

Me: Hey :D Bored you say?

Nikita: Nothing much just excited about today's function. You know Kiarra is dancing today?

Me: Oh yeah I know.

Nikita: Kiarra and you again friends?

Me: No :b

Nikita: You really love her right?

Me: Nikita you know what I seriously love that girl. It's because of my fault that such thing happened and I really feel guilty for whatever I have done. I broke her heart and I know how it must have pained her. I am really very sorry for everything.

Nikita: I don't know what happened but did you apologise?

Me: I did a lot of times but she is not going come back now. ☹

And if she is ready to mend things back this time I am not letting her go anyway. Many say you'll get better but how do I say them I want nobody. I just want her back.

Nikita: You go and clear out things then.

Me: I am scared a bit. I don't know what's there in her mind about me. But if she is kind of ready I have no problem.

Nikita: Okay hope everything gets well soon. Anyway I'll talk to you later, I have to go.

Me: okay bye.

She would understand me now, was a thought stronger than all the things that were keeping me away from her.

This was what I prepared. I made up this plan because I thought may be after reading all this Kiarra would still feel I had feelings for her and she would try to contact me. She would once again think upon my rude behaviour. If my words have affected her then my words would heal her.

This time there was a difference.

Now the next thing Nikita got to do is show this chat to Kiarra or take screenshot of our chat and send it to her. The choice was hers but this was to be done before Annual day program.

I knew I was mean to her. I used her to get Kiarra.

In school I saw Kiarra standing near the pillar with her dance group.

I watched something unusual every time I looked at her. She was staring at me and it was something odd at that time.

I understood that Nikita had executed the plan.

After the assembly the council members were instructed to move to head in charges for taking their duties. I along with three others were given the duty to manage things and audience in the VVIP section.

In My Eternity

We four of us bent forward at the entrance to welcome the dignified man. The whole crowd stood up and clapped as he entered the arena near the front row.

It was such a pleasure to welcome the former Finance Minister of the country P. Chidambaram as the chief guest of the occasion.

His body guards left him and then we four accompanied the Chief Guest, Principal Ma'am, Director Sir, Secretary of the school and other authorities to their seats. As they took their seats we all four went and stood near the front stage.

The moment came when Mr. P Chidambaram came on the dais to deliver the speech. Everyone grabbed their seats tight to hear his thoughts. It was one of the awaited speeches for the evening for the crowd. He came to enlighten the crowd with his words of wisdom.

His speech was much imposing than any other speeches I have ever heard.

As his speech was ended, we accompanied the guests towards their seats and it was our last job of the evening. I was privileged to serve the man.

I left the rest of the program and went to find Kiarra in the school building. I roamed around her green room without any purpose.

I went down to the ground as I had a call from my parents. They were here too for the Annual Day. In between I met Nikita.

"What did she say? What was her reaction?"

"I showed her our chats. She read that three times. She even asked me to send the whole chat in screenshots. And then she called Kavya. She also read it and both stood completely blank."

"Okay anything more?"

"Till now nothing but let's see what she has to say to me? She would definitely give me some reply to those screenshots."

"Then forward me your chat please Nikita."

"Okay but I want something in return."

"A treat?" she demanded.

"Done" I confirmed.

I watched the last show with my parents and that was too her dance.

I went to the exit with my parents to leave them.

I ran towards the students parking then to wait for her. I stood for five minutes there and then Vinni came to me. After my Breakup I had never spoken to her neither gave her any expression that something has happened because of her.

She requested me for a photo. I denied at first but then she came closer with her mobile phone. We both were alone in the parking.

I gave a smile to the phone. She came even closer to me on the second click. As she was clicking, I heard a crush of leaves from the other path on the way for parking. I thought it would be a rat or a squirrel passing by.

In My Eternity

I turned to see whether really there was someone behind the repetitive noise. I saw Kiarra standing there with her hopes crushed once again. She had always wanted me to be like this to her and not to any girl.

She turned back quickly in anger and moved on.

My first impulse was to run behind her but my legs had gone weak.

"Kiarra, wait" I called her. I tried to find a way out in between the parked two wheelers. Vinni held my hand and stopped me from leaving her. I helped my hand out of her hand and then ran towards her.

"Kiarra wait and listen to me" I shouted at her back. She quickly covered her half path towards the school building. I ran faster to catch her. "Kiarra it is nothing like that believe me." I stopped her but she carried on with her footsteps.

She got mixed in the crowd soon and then I left.

Vinni had ruined it all over again.

It was really hard to throw away the thought of what happened in the evening. It astonished me that she came back.

I went home and then upstairs to the terrace with my head phones, played the playlist that reminded me of her and gave me answers. The person who gave me unexplained happiness became my source of never ending sadness.

After Days

My heart still had feelings for her. In these months I contacted her several times but she didn't reply. In school, I stared at her when she was not looking and then suddenly when she looked at me I removed my eyes from her pretending I am busy. It happen the other way too. I loved it when she kept looking at me and then I catch her eyes. I wished I could just crawl into her head and ask what she thought about me while she stood staring.

Our shadows crossed several times in the school but with heads down, we never looked in each other's eyes. Nobody around could ever make up who broke whose heart.

I slept late at night every day. I remember staying up until midnight chatting with her was hard to do but now chatting with none and still not sleeping till mid night had became a bad habit. Not everyone deserved to be the reason behind my sleepless night.

I stalked her from the day she had left me. I saved her contacts in Krishh's phone just to see her whatsapp profile pictures. Nevertheless our mutual friends would come and talk about her. Kiarra did this and did that. In my trouble I received messages from my friends. They were sympathetically teasing me.

I was sick of crying, tired of trying yes I was smiling but inside I was dying. I cried a river and it was time to build a bridge over the river.

It was time to be happy again.

In My Eternity

Funny, how strangers who enter your life as friends mean so much to you at a point of time. All of a sudden they make all the bad things fall at right place for you. Share things with you.

Never let you forget about them. The familiar stranger makes you text almost 24*7 and you have no idea when the stars came and went. You open your heart to them and share every single thing of your life.

You remain in their magnetic field all the time. They pull you closer to them. And you get so used to it that you can't stay away from them. They make you believe that you are the right one for them. They fall for you from the beginning and try to make you fall with them.

But just at a point of time you just can't stop loving them.

But just at a point of time you have them completely in you clutch.

But just at the point of life when you can't live without them, they just walk out of your life like you didn't mean anything to them.

But just at the point of life when you actually start trusting love, your trust is badly shattered.

You are said that we can't talk anymore. And then you stand at that edge of life, when you read the texts which used to bring smile and gave a blush to your cheeks, now makes you sink down and water in your eyes.

It tears up your heart when you see them or hear their name.

On the eve of 31st December I decided to close her chapter, a feeling that she is in another world and better not to interrupt her.

It's not like how I used to see things she also saw them the same way. I need to make my own path away from her. I need to keep myself moving on.

Sometimes some people are not just meant to stay in our time always or for a point of time. The outcomes are changes and these changes bring you so much to tolerate, you need to stand up high in your situation. You cannot think to look down once.

But these changes for each time would be saving your life. It would lead to a better world in the end.

I was not a sentimental person but what all happened between us meant something to me.

Taking revenge with Vinni was not in my plans. I was just damn tired of everything. Ultimately Karma is my God. I left it to Karma.

I deleted our messages and photos. I paused at a photo, my eyes were watery by the time I removed my thumb from the delete option. Bhavya's picture smiled back at me.

. . .

So that day we ended up with our counselling sessions in school. Throughout the year representatives from different parts of India, and around the world came to portray their colleges and universities. They helped us know about their culture, courses offered and much more.

My friends were confident with what they wanted to pursue in life and from where. Some were preparing for SAT examinations, CLAT, CPT, some wanted colleges through their merit result and rest didn't know what they wanted to do.

I was amongst the rest. Always, I have been jumping and tossing with my aim from one end to another end. Till 7th class I wanted to become a Doctor and then suddenly I watched myself as an Engineer in the coming years. When I first met Physics, Chemistry and Biology separately I decided to opt for commerce in eleventh because Physics never went into my head. I only understood gravity in cartoons. Then I decided to become a CA.

Somewhere I think falling in love with her and messing up with things have deviated me from my goals. They had come to a screeching halt, because of my horrendous decision that affected nobody but me.

In all these years I never left my dream of becoming a cricketer or an Actor.

But this is so far the toughest decision I had to make in my life. What if I start with Acting or cricket now? And then in the later years I won't succeed. What if I don't play International cricket or I don't work with great movie directors. I will be working somewhere in these fields but what if I don't get the fame and lots of money. And then these fields would be useless to continue with.

I talk on this with my father a hundred times. He never says no to me on anything whether it is choosing CA or Cricket or anything. He wants me to go for what I can achieve.

When I looked inside me I founded greed. Greed for a lot of money and name in the society, I want people to run behind me for photographs and signatures.

May be what I have seen in these years with celebrities have created this sort of awakening in my mind.

I want to fulfil this greed someday. I have a thirst of it right from the beginning and I know education to its extent won't take me to it. Knowing this fact I have given education a pivotal position every time.

I have always feared what if I didn't study, what if I didn't get good marks? But nothing of such sort has mattered in the end. Nobody has asked me in which class do you failed your maths exam and how much did you score in a particular subject in some class.

I remember when I joined a cricket club back in 5th class. I represented that club for 4 years. I gave state as well as national trials time and again. Those who played worse than me got selected and I remained aback. This was only because Politics interfered here. My friends told me how their father misused their powers and gave bribes to the coaches. They had asked me to do the same but I never wanted my dad to do all such things. I wanted to play it fair. But when all such things increased day by day and I gave up. I left Cricket.

It was of no use when you put your 100% and you benefit nothing out of it.

For this reason I never put my hands into Acting. I didn't wish to fight this kind of world.

I make out, I can get any degree by studying and I am really confident about that thing but somewhere my heart asked for some things to be altered. I never liked studies.

I still desire to become a Cricketer or an Actor. I am ready to work my ass off for any of the two things but all I want is someone to hold my hand and show me the right path or take me to world where fair chances are welcomed.

Sometimes I think I am the one who is going to do it for me. A voice always rises from inside but my actions fear the execution.

18!

"Only two months more and you will be through with your 12th boards. I hope you have started preparing for your exams and if not start from today" Sir concluded the first day of school after the New Year day.

It was one of the worst things to hear in those days. It lets you to jog your memory that the school days would be over soon. The school was actually over and 12th class students were given a preparation leave until the first paper of the boards. The school arranged revision and doubt solving classes every day. Students were also allowed to come to school for self study.

I prepared my time-table for the revision. I pinned it adjacent to my rules in the room. I got through the rules once again and laughed. Ultimately I had wrecked them all.

Day by day I gave considerable amount of time to my studies. Only few attended the classes rest enjoyed their studies at home. Didn't they love their school?

The School was never in my list of favorite place. I didn't like to visit this place but later it became my second home. I decided to come and enjoy the last days of the school. I counted for how many days I have to wear the uniform more. I hated it throughout my school life, but it became one of the best dresses in the entire wardrobe ultimately. I had realised in the last days that it was not bad at all on me. The alarm also didn't trouble much in the morning to get up for school.

Farewell day I stopped her to improve things with a hope that she had forgiven me. "Hey, I want to talk to you."

"No you don't" the reply was quick. High school mates in the corridors stared at me thinking, why after so much time I am still not over with her.

"Please don't come near me okay? I hate you" she said. Her tone was irritable; her voice that used to speak to me with laughter and now is used only to show hate. But I knew she wasn't her.

With agony in her eyes she left me, she left me with her bittersweet memories once again.

· · ·

The fact was hard to believe for my parents that I would become an adult after two hours. I was taking dinner with the family.

"Munda bada ho gya ab jaldi se iski shaadi krado" My grandma said.

"Dadi abhi sirf 18 ka hua hu abhi kaha se shadi aur waise bhi mujhe shaadi krke koi raula ni pana h.

She was the only one concerned about it in the whole family. Being the eldest son of the family my Grandma wanted to see me getting married and then go to Heaven.

I did not like the idea of marriage. I had already told my family members that I am not going to marry in any case and gave them my reasons too. I revised them again at the dining table that day.

1. I want to lead tension free life. No wife, no children no problems. I will enjoy my vacations with my friends.
2. I will earn alone and eat alone. I won't share my bucks with anyone. I do not want to become poor.
3. Once you marry you are finished. You live in a cage and there is no way out. You are trapped.
4. There are chances of divorce in the future and what will I do if she would ask me for my property or anything.
5. I hate shopping.
6. It is surely going to kill my life with other girls. I can never make friends with opposite gender and even if I do she will stalk me. My freedom would be gone.
7. I can't eat food from any other hand. I love my mom's hand taken food.
8. I don't want any Saas-Bahu stories in my life. I don't want my life to convert in one of the Ekta Kapoor's serial.
9. Above all even if I decide to marry I would marry on several conditions. First love marriage, second if I am a billionaire or something like that and third I would go with the court marriage. No band baaja and baraat."

Their reaction was the same like always.

I was sleepy. I took my dinner and went upstairs. I wanted to go and sleep but I waited for the clock to struck 12 fast. My eyes were burning.

Meanwhile I arranged my bag according to revision classes for tomorrow and then put chocolates in the bag.

In My Eternity

The time elapsed slowly and I was getting sleepy quickly. Still there were ten minutes more. I gave up and went to my bed and slept.

I heard my phone's ringtone ringing continuously. I was half asleep. The phone ringtone told me that the time had come. It was Nikita who was calling me.

After I hung her phone my family members came in my room.

I was out of the bed. I quickly accepted their wishes. Like always Krishh was not there to wish me. He would always wish me at 23:59 of my birthday date.

This time whistles and beep of horns woke me up. It was boisterous. There can't be any traffic jams in a colony and someone was doing it on purpose. Then there was burning of crackers. I went up to the window to see who was making the noise.

I had never in my life would have expected this. It was blue sort of thing. My friends were standing in front of the house.

I wore my slippers and then went down. All the gates of the house were already unlocked as if my family members were also part of the whole plan.

I opened the main gate of the house. As I stepped out and was closing it behind something was shot straight at my head. It hurt. My hair got sticky and wet.

"Aaaooochh" I turned to see what more my friends have got for me. I saw all five standing in a semi circle with an egg in their hand each. I saw Krishh too.

I had no option than to run away. I had closed the door behind me. The only option I could see was to break the wall and run. I was trapped.

I did not say anything. After a moment of silence they put their egg in their polythene.

"Chill bro we won't do anything." The peace treaty was signed. All of them headed towards me and wished me Happy Birthday with a warm hug and hard 18 bumps by each on the back.

"I was expecting this." I said although I didn't have any clue. As I cut the cake and they sang the birthday song.

After everything was done they smashed their eggs at me. Around 10 eggs were hit on me. My mummy who was witnessing all this from the balcony asked them to stop. Still they had 2-3 eggs each in their polythene.

My father was also standing in the balcony with her. He did not say anything rather he was enjoying the whole thing.

"Uncle what are we suppose to do with the left over eggs?" Raj asked. "Do you want to eat an omelette?" Raj stood there thinking as if my dad would really cook it for him. "Then finish it." He completed.

They began again until all were over. Eggs came from everywhere. Fortunately my pull-over had protected my chest and body while I used my hand to save the face. That was not something I came down for. I was hurt by the eggs so much that I almost cried.

They were not yet finished. They applied cake over my body.

Due to their surprises the whole colony was awake and out by the noise. Hardly anyone had slept. They all stood in their balconies watching the drama. Some wished me from a distance.

They entire area in front of my house was covered with pieces of egg.

I thanked them for such a big surprise. It was the best birthday night ever in my life.

When I went to the bed I found it tough to sleep, my body was paining from head to toe. Still I felt like I was beaten up by those rotten eggs.

Through all these years I failed to understand to react to my friends, who sing birthday song for me. It was the worst feeling in front of everybody. But now it was for the last time they were singing for me in the class.

In school when the classes got over I got ready with my shots and Green school house T-shirt to run the last race for my club.

Today was a special day. My birthday and last race for my house and being a captain this time I wanted the first position. Every year the Athletics events were the most awaited on my side.

When I got ready I warmed up by practicing shots on the basketball court with Raj. Today he was my opponent too.

One of my friends who had been running races with me every year was sitting in the crowd this time. He had a leg injury. He was my best contender. No race was a race without him. I missed him in my last race for the club.

He had earlier told me that the easiest way of winning a race is that hold your urine during the race and then see how you run. You wouldn't run for winning, rather you would run so fast only because you want to get in to the washroom and pee. Create a good force. It was sarcastic but it was absolutely a sporty thing, it worked all the time.

Soon the announcement for 400m Relay was made and we both ran towards our spots. I fixed my army for the Relay.

"The fastest will start and the quickest will end it. The plan goes simple. All the best and give out everything for your captain."

One among the four of us stood at the starting point and the one who was running second on his place after a space of 100metres from the beginning point. Today I wanted to be the 'Flying Sikh' for my house.

Number 3 and I stood by the sidelines witnessing our contestants. Our sports head took the whistle in his mouth. The crowd stood still and desperate to watch the last race of the session.

"On your Mark, Get set, *whistles*"

Sagar took a good pick up but in the end he was second to handover the baton to number 2. I appreciated his efforts among his competitors. Number 2 made it a bit worse as he was the third to hand over the baton to number 3.

I stood in my lane because it was my turn to end the race and eventually run down to the washroom and urinate.

It happens always with me before starting my race. I feel so nervous. My legs quiver.

Number 3 maintained the position. Before I got the green baton in my hand my friends from Red and yellow house had already started their journey towards the finishing point. I was some 15-20 metres behind when I got the baton in my hand.

It was just 100m and all I could see was the circular path I had to cover. I heard the crowd shouting and cheering.

I ran with all my strength towards glory. I gave up all the energy in me to reach to the point.

I gathered so much strength that in the half way I was running parallel with the Blue house participant. I was thinking to quicken my steps even more just then I felt something losing downwards.

My legs could not hold down more. I got unbalanced and fell down on my face.

I felt a jerk inside my body; it seemed all the food I took in my lunch was in my throat. I had the ground dirt all over my body and in my mouth.

There was boo from the crowd.

Laid on the ground I saw him inching towards the second place. I lost where I was. I gave up and patted hard on the ground with my face downside.

"Ujjawal get up and run" Raj shouted from the sidelines. Though his Red house had won the race already but he wanted me to come second.

I looked behind. He was not too far away from me. I summoned all what was left in me and ran with all the blood marks on my chin, elbows, palms and knee.

I ran fast, and I didn't allow the one behind me to cover my lead and in the end I came third. I had a chance to win but

God was not so kind to let me win on my birthday. I lay on the ground as I finished it.

My coach and other participants patted on my back for getting up and finishing the race. It was a nice gesture.

All thanks to Raj.

My friends came with the medical kit and then they applied detol and stuffs over my body. It pained and burnt. I never wanted this to happen on my birthday.

I cleared the field and then went inside the washroom. Not to pee but I vomited. All the food came out at once.

I dressed up with the new pair of clothes for the evening. I cut the second cake of the day with my classmates at dinner. And how can a party be over without a drink. After all I had reached the magical and legal age of eighteen. I was finally an adult and now I had the permission to do everything which I had been doing illegally.

We all childhood friends shared a bottle.

The third cake was cut at 11'o clock. I went out for a dinner with my family.

I focused hard on my subjects after my birthday. The fear of 12th boards kept me away from the socialising. Getting an aggregate of 95 or above in the boards was my aim because I wanted to pursue my further studies from Delhi University and I was fully determined to achieve it. The thought of going to Delhi University nourished the seed in my heart and became an intense desire to be fulfilled.

I kept going to the school for revision classes. Though I had revised my whole course twice but then Basketball and school food would pull me to the school. I had hunger for both. On the other hand Teacher's arranged run through papers twice in a week for our practice and managing time.

On Republic day came the results. We stood 4th. It was the third consecutive time. The other council members teased me. Finally my duty as a captain was over. It was real fun. I bunked lectures and helped some of my mates to do so. That was something power could do.

Earlier I counted the number of months on fingers but now I could count the number of days left in the school.

Was I dreaming all this or is this real? Fourteen years in the school just flew so quickly. I can still remember my first step in Sri Sathya Sai Vidya Vihar.

I hadn't wanted these days to go so fast.

I wanted to go back to those times once again.

Chapter 19

Eternities

"Ujjawal, today at night will you stay at my home?" Raj called me on the eve of first day of financial year.

"What is the special occasioning my friend?" I asked.

"The special day is tomorrow" he said merrily. I chortled.

"We'll sort out some old things" he demanded.

"Eh! What." I stood bemused.

"I mean doubts. Come home and teach me theory and I'll sort all your practical problems."

"Done! Meet you at 10 then."

I took dinner and packed up my bag with the required books. When I reached his home he was already buried in the Accounts book mugging up theory.

I also started with the theory. We both sat on the opposite side of the wall not facing each other. He was time and again texting someone on the phone but I didn't care to ask.

We studied without a word till 11:30 when he interrupted the silence.

"I am hungry. I hadn't had my dinner yet. Let's hang out somewhere."

"Find something in the kitchen. I am not interested in going out right now" I said half dead.

"There is nothing there. My parents are out and mom told me to take dinner outside."

"Then you should have taken it when I was not here. You can't study sincerely huh. Can you?"

"Shut up and let's go. We'll come in half-n-hour and then study as much as you wish to. The whole night is yours."

"Who would keep his restaurant open for you at this time?"

"I am looking for some street food and there is only one place you could find it right now?"

He gave me some clothes as I was in my shorts and night tee. Then we both travelled 4miles to Rajwada to get his tummy filled.

He wished me Happy Birthday on the way as the clock struck twelve. For he was the only one who would give me reasons to stay even when I didn't wanted too. He circuitously kept me close to her memories.

I poked him from behind. The Bike got unbalanced. We were going to get bash in a car coming opposite to us from the other lane but Raj managed the handle.

We heard the car stopped behind us in furious breaks. The driver looked at us through the side mirror. Raj said something fowl to him. He got out and started chasing us. Raj then drove the Bike in speed.

When we reached he ordered food. The Pav-Bhaji made my mouth watery so I took one plate with him. When we were finished we decided to leave.

He took the wrong route to home.

"Aren't we finished yet? Is there anything more?" I asked.

"Not more than you can ask for." I didn't understand what he said. I remained quiet to his response. I slept on his shoulders.

He stopped in front of a public park near the Highway. We had come far way after travelling 10 minutes more.

I was curious to know what he had for me at one in the night. The park didn't have anything nor did he have anything with him.

There were no guards protecting the gates and they were too high to climb, so we decided to jump.

He jumped to the other side of the two meter high fence and I followed him.

"They are still not here." He said. He went afar and then on his phone called the 'they' who were not there when we had already arrived.

"We have to wait for fifteen minutes more." He said as he came after attending the call.

"For what?" I asked out of interest.

"Shaant baithega? He shouted.

"Who am I to waste my time for you? Give me the keys I have to study. I'll come and take you tomorrow in the morning." I replied. He was exacerbating my study mood.

"I should say these words rather." He paused for a minute staring at me in disdain. "Please it is a matter of half n hour more" He pleaded.

I went to one of the swing and played songs while he roamed in the empty garden.

I don't know for whom we were waiting and for what? In time I played answers I had just mugged up in my mind. I revised accounts.

Eventually after twenty more minutes in time I saw some light in front of the gates. Someone came. As Raj saw it he asked me to remain where I was.

He walked towards the garden gates to address the 'they' which came. It gave me some relief that we were going to get home soon now.

I was trying to see who was there but I could not find a way. The bush in between me and the garden gates never helped me to look beyond it. I called Raj after two minutes but he cut the phone.

I saw three silhouettes coming towards me. I stood up in jerk. I felt my body traumatised as I was confirmed that yes they were them.

I unstated why Raj was so hungry in the night and why he had taken the wrong route to home.

Our eyes met like it used to do before. I felt lost in front of the one, who meant the world to me. She was dressed in strength and all she wanted this time was dignity.

I don't know why after giving up I still prized her? Things were clear that she doesn't feel the same for me. The problem was that as much I can't force her to love me I can't stop myself from loving her. I felt paralysingly numb. Within a span of time all the memories flashbacked my mind.

It didn't occur to me to question what was happening. What they were doing? What on earth was going on? I could make nothing out of why they were here. No matter what but I was enjoying the strange pleasure.

"You both are over thinking right now. Please Don't. I and Kavya have cleared out all what happened between you people and you both just be like before." Raj interrupted the silence.

"Ujjawal dude, Raj bhaiya will tell you everything and Kiarra I'll talk to you. For now you both just understand that misunderstanding won between your love and friendship".

Things changed in those months. Kavya became a love guru. I appreciated her last line.

They drew apart from the scene making room for us.

For I have never said a no. I wanted my life to invest on her again.

Does she still love me? Or does she not? Anyway if she does she'll be mine now and if she doesn't I'll innate that she never was. I was ready to accept anything today. Even when she was not mine I had a fear of losing her. I waited.

She heisted and stole eye contacts with me. It was a magical scene, in which I was put into, completely by chance.

I gazed at her.

"Happy Birthday Kiarra" I finally spoke.

In My Eternity

She came towards me and I too moved forward. We hugged. It was uncomfortable after all this time. I felt the warmth. That warmth healed everything. She was beautiful from the heart.

Something in the strength of dark happened; leaving me agreed.

"I am sorry Kiarra. I am really very sorry for everything."

She remained quiet and didn't move. She was listening to my heart. For once that time I could not define what love was. All I could say is that sometimes it is even sexier to touch the soul of a woman than to touch her body.

Our love for each other never died. It was just temporarily murdered by misinterpretation, ignorance, behaviour, attitude, ego and that Vinni.

In a couple of minutes they both arrived. Raj had a white box in his hand and Kavya had a bottle of fruit beer. We all four sat in a circle on the ground. Raj opened the box.

It was a Birthday cake for her.

"Ujjawal I said know I'll give you the best gift. So here is your pending Birthday gift." He pointed towards Kiarra while Kavya did the rest of unpacking of the box.

"And Kiarra here is your Birthday gift." She rejoined, not put out for a moment.

At last I had got my friends back again. Heroes are found in the most improbable places they say. I had not in my life expected that Raj could do anything like this for me. It was time to celebrate us.

She cut the cake and Kavya opened the bottle of fruit beer. She took the first piece towards my mouth. I cut a small piece of it and applied it all over her face. We shared the cake and finished the whole bottle.

We all four laid on the grass looking at the stars not worrying about the problems we were going through and not thinking what the world can have all for us in the future.

We did not discuss about what happened before.

This was probably the best moment of my life.

I decided not share it with anyone. I told them to keep this all in between us.

"It will be our secret forever." She whispered.

I never wanted to get back in a relationship with her. I was scared to lose her again. I wanted my love story to end just being best friends again. She accepted my friendship approval.

The second time things made more sense.

"Ujjawal you don't want to study now? Now your time is not wasting?" He teased me.

I checked the time on the watch. It was almost four. I never wished to go but I didn't want history to repeat again.

We gathered all the mess we had created and threw it on one side.

First we left Kiarra and Kavya outside their society. It was a two minute drive down the road in front of the park.

They have told their parents that they are on a Night Stay with their old school mates for they have planned a surprise for Kiarra's Birthday.

While getting home I asked Raj about the whole thing.

"Kavya and I cleared things a month before. We were just waiting for the right moment. You know I had your facebook password? I read your and Kiarra's chat months before. And Nakul was just a show off. He was lying to you about the kissing part. They went but only for Kiarra's treat. I gathered all the info from Naksh my friend at club who went with Nakul. I trusted him because he is my friend from childhood. I accidently saw a picture in his phone which had Nakul, Kiarra and him. And Vinni poisoned her ear that's it."

The things were beginning to get clear.

I wondered on the way home, had they any real or universal sense to my breakup, it was merely a whimsical.

I felt guilty for blaming her without any proof. The thing I was fighting for with myself was achieved so easily. In the end I just regretted the chances I didn't take, and the decisions I was too afraid to make. I never thought because of all such things I would look back on that laughter and cry. But now it was time to be happy again. Kiarra I know and Kiarra I have felt can never do this. I knew that well.

The road which nearly seemed to be an end was a new turn.

6th April 2015. I looked in the mirror. I saw an 18 years old boy standing in front of me. He was dressed in strength, dignity and respect for society, a student fed with morals, Character, Honesty, and Responsibility; ready to convert opportunities into goals with will and potential.

For the last time I was dressed in my school uniform.

I frequently asked a question to my mom "Main bada kab banunga?" Every time she would say, "you will know yourself." I used to think it to be age number 18. Perhaps because people talk about that age so much. At 18, you leave some places and find a new way for yourself. People say you gain conscience.

It's been three months to the magical age of 18 but nothing of this sort happened to me. Everything seems the same as before.

When I looked behind recollecting instances, I found that I already have these qualities. I don't have to wait to be an adult.

From the past few years, the desire to express myself has budded. I do realise somewhere that I am becoming different from my mates. I do not see things like I used to when I was about 15. When Krishh comes up with his thoughts to me, then I look back and I find myself under the same spell. But those things don't excite me anymore.

For the last time I took my nib in hand to write something from school. I jumped up high in the air as the 12th boards were over. Finally the moment has come. There was relief.

So I walked down in those corridors memorising everything – the classroom, the dining hall, the toilets, the desk and memories of all those years that passed away so quickly.

When no one was watching I took a slide on the elephant slide. The last time I slid on it was six years ago.

I then hopped onto the See-Saw adjacent to elephant slide. I always feared to go on a see-saw with a fat kid. It was no fun then. I recalled how my friends and I played together. This time there was no one to pull me up again.

In My Eternity

I remember hiding behind the buses, behind the trees and bushes, and in the washrooms while we played Hide and Seek. The game taught me that I don't have to hide there and wait for people to conceal me. I just need to get up, put in my own efforts and take hold of the game. I think life is all about this.

I recalled the fear of sitting in front of the Saraswati Temple. It was one of the punishments that every child in Sathya Sai never wanted to get. Once you were there, the whole school will come to see you and laugh at you.

I saw the Basketball court and remembered my last match for the school. The football ground in which I fell a hundred time and then got up. The ground in which I ran and won races for my club. All it was to take a step forward to take thousands of steps ahead. The road in front of me was solely mine.

And as I move on, I recalled thousands of memories from each and every corner of the school.

Here I am, leaving for the last time. There would be no coming back, no sleeping with the books, no more sports periods, no more laughing over with classmates on a stupid thing, no more playing pranks, no more stealing glances when the teacher asked the question, no more thinking about the fantasies of the world while having prayers, no more sharing chocolates and chewing gums with friends, no more coming late to the class and then standing out of the class in punishment and enjoying that time.

There would be no more polishing shoes the night before, no more taking out the school uniform from the wardrobe, no more riding to the school.

I recalled some of my embarrassing moments in the school. Slipping in the mud in front my crush in 10th standard was the most humiliating thing that happened to me. Peeing in the class when I was in my Junior Montessori, though none of them would remember it but I know I remained in the wetness during the whole school hiding it from the teachers and everybody.

And some heroic moments like winning the Basketball matches by close margins in the recess, Principal ma'am deluding me by calling me ShahRukh Khan in front of the whole class, but asking me to cut my messy hair.

And it was in the higher classes when I realised that I need not feel sorry for my faults and flaws and punishments were just another way to make fun out of it. Good marks were never a measure of love the teachers had for us. I learned that we need not be in a rat race with our friends for better grades.

With every class new relations were made and some were broken. Friends changed after long summer vacations. Some become fatter, some develops the richness on their face, some change their hairstyle, they come with new bags and pencil boxes to the school, and new faces pop up on the benches where you used to sit before the vacations

We won't remember everything we studied here, but was taught to us. The dates of wars, the trigonometry formulas, polynomials, the present and past participle, the economic reforms; all we will take with us are memories of this place. Even if we forget the names, we'll never forget the faces.

All we would remember are those tussles we had or witnessed between the school boys, the lyrics we played a thousand times in our mind during the lectures, the times when we bunked classes, the times when we locked our best friends in the washroom and getting ourselves trapped, we would remember who threw the best parties in the class, who had a silly answer to every serious question that the teacher asked, who entertained the whole class, who was the smartest, and who had the most cynical attitude.

I stepped out of the school at the gate and turned around to see the edifice behind me. It evoked my mind how I used to race to the class with my mates after getting down from the school van. And then suddenly it seemed like some energy pushed me towards the school again, it again gave me the power to chase down to the class. But it was time to leave, to end an eternity and begin a new one.

7th April 2015.

And as I walk around the house; it's difficult for me to settle. There is nothing out of place, and it feels different. All the things are kept settled on the right place. I wanted these things to unsettle for a time like it used to be before when he was there Like before not everything was left touched and moved. The TV remote, the newspaper, the keys, the toys, the sofa cover all were in their proper places now. These untouched things left me touched and felt. I missed those familiar comforts of my life. Now there was no 'he'.

He was there with me till last April. As usual we talked, we ate, we fought and we played. But as the calendar changed its page, he left me. He walks beside me unheard and unseen but I still miss him. This feeling was compassion beyond words, beyond language, and this compassion arose from the fact that there is no separation at all.

The only difference today is that now I talk, I eat, I fight and I play with his commemoration.

Today is his Birthday in another year but same date. Papa and I went to the Thalassemia society and donated blood. Losing a child was something that my family and I have been through and we never wanted anyone to suffer the same loss.

I think we don't age by years but by stories.

About the Author

Ujjawal Pahwa, a 19 year old, from Indore has finished his high school in 2015. He is currently doing his under graduation in B.com (Honors) in Indore. His hobbies are writing, photography, sports and shaping his dreams. He loves to do charity in his free time and dreams of contributing something big to the society.

Get in a conversation with the Author through his official Facebook ID, at https://www.facebook.com/ujjawal.pahwa

You can also write to him at inmyeternityauthor@gmail.com

Printed in the United States
By Bookmasters